42 Avenue of the Americas

ALSO BY VICTOR KLINE

BOOKS
Rough Justice
The House at Anzac Parade
The Golden Dagger Mysteries (Contributor)

PLAYS
The Rehabilitation of God
Love.Com
The Legionnaire
The Salsa Lesson
Sex, Death & Chocolates
Doctor Faustus Sings
Hedda Gabler (Translation)
The Fruit Bats of Charters Towers

42 AVENUE OF THE AMERICAS

VICTOR KLINE

Frances Allen Pty Limited

WITH SPECIAL THANKS TO

Dr. Michael Gliksman, Dr. Katharine Kline, Karen
Makhoul, Belinda Marques,
Jennifer Philip and Jane Edwina Seymour.

ISBN-13: 978-0-947245-10-8

To Katharine Kline, the love of all my lives

1.

Joe Stalin was an interesting character, to say the least. He ran a shoeshine business in the Pitt Street Mall. That was brave. In Australia no-one did that. Australians like to shine their own shoes. However that didn't stop Joe.

'You'd be wasting your time,' the other homeless guys tried to tell him.

But no successful businessman ever got successful by listening to the 'wisdom' of others. Joe knew what he wanted and had the *chutzpah* to pull it off. In a relatively short space of time he had a thriving business.

With every shoeshine there was a little advice, if that's what you wanted. Most came for the advice. I know I did. Though you had to admit he gave a mighty fine shine. I couldn't scuff my shoes for two weeks afterwards, even if I tried; which was a problem if I needed another consultation.

The rumor around town was, he had been

Pete A. Vanderveer's marketing guru, back in the day, when Pete first made the Bloomberg Billionaires' List. They said Joe had a lot to do with Pete's success. But one day he just took off, left Vanderveer without so much as an explanation. He spent the next few years tramping around America, only to end up back in his home town of Sydney, broke and homeless.

What brought on such a lifestyle choice, no-one could say. What his real name was, no-one could be sure. Indeed whether there was a shred of truth to the whole story, no-one could really testify. But the homeless of Sydney and Joe's customers wanted to believe it.

He was certainly well loved. One time he went missing for a couple of weeks, and the other homeless guys organized search parties. They hunted all around the city for him. When he didn't show up they decided he must have passed on. To show their love and respect they staged a memorial service in Martin Place.

Joe found it touching, not to mention a little amusing, to walk in on his own funeral, just as Willy the Wastrel was saying a prayer for the deliverance of his soul.

I guess he did well enough in his one man business. He always had customers, and most, like me, gave him more than the going rate. We'll never know of course because, like most successful capitalists, he didn't pay any tax.

He also had very few overheads, paid no

super, salaries or insurance, worked in the open air so he had no rent, and kept his business portable, so he could beat a quick retreat when the City of Sydney Rangers came into the Mall.

I last consulted Joe a couple of months back. I felt I was at the crossroads of life. I had no idea which road to take, or even where the roads led.

'I'm feeling stuck, Joe,' I told him as I sat on the little portable canvas seat his customers used.

I looked down at Joe sitting cross-legged on the ground, sorting his polishes and brushes. His flexible, youthful body didn't seem to match that worldly and weather beaten face. I had often wondered how old he was. He could have been anything from 35 to 55. It was impossible to tell.

'Stuck, Vic? What sort of stuck?' he asked, his voice a gentle lilt, the vowels falling somewhere between Manhattan and the eastern suburbs of Sydney.

'I'm at the crossroads of life,' I told him.

'Ah,' he nodded. His broad smile showed one left incisor missing, and one bottom tooth, casualties perhaps of his time on the road. 'You know, we're all there with you.'

'I'm sorry?'

'We're all at the crossroads of life. Everyone is always at the crossroads of life.'

'You think so?' I asked.

'Sure,' he said. 'You tell me one time in your life you didn't have to make a choice about something. One time when you could just sit back and say: "Yep I've got it all together, I know where I am, and I know where I'm going".'

'So you're at the crossroads too?'

'I sure am,' he replied as he started to put the polish on my shoes. He was thorough, moving systematically about the shoe so as not to miss a patch.

'What decision do you have to make?' I asked.

He smiled at me again, this time broader than before, revealing another missing tooth.

'Right now I have to decide whether to answer your questions, and perhaps set us both on a path from which there will be no going back, or to leave you in your state of confusion and flee the mall.'

Was he joking? You could never tell with Joe. He said everything in the same re-assuring, lilting voice, so that in the end it didn't seem to matter either way.

'You must think I have some mighty big decisions to make?' I asked.

'You undoubtedly do.'

'Have you become a mind reader as well, Joe?'

'Not at all. It's just that everyone always has big decisions to make. Just like the crossroads. Always at the crossroads, always big decisions to make.'

'You make it sound very dramatic.' I couldn't help laughing.

He laughed too. 'It *is* dramatic, Vic. Life is dramatic. Everyone is always just one decision away from changing the world.'

'I don't think I'm quite ready to change the world,' I told him.

'Too big a job?' He stopped polishing and waved his hand at the lunchtime crowds in the Pitt Street Mall.

'Way too big,' I said, as I watched every possible type of humanity, surge past and around us.

Just then a young man stopped nearby. He was big, tattooed and wore a singlet that showed off his bulging muscles. He looked like he was on his way to *The Yagoona Bodypunch Gym*. Whilst pointing a very long finger far too close to my face, he said to his friends:

'See it is bastards like this one.' Then directly to me: 'Shame on you, mate. Taking advantage of the unemployed, like this. God will smote you, mate!'

I was amazed. Had he really said "smote"? Was I the first person in 2000 years to fall under the threat of a good smoting? His accent was very thick. Maybe I had misheard. But no, there was no doubt. For he obligingly repeated himself.

'Smote you, mate!'

I was also confused. What was his problem? Joe was trying to earn a living shining shoes and I was helping him earn that living. Surely God would take no exception to that. But then I remembered how differently people can see the same scene.

I wanted to explain the error in his thinking,

but he was very big, and looked like he was just about to hang me up and use me as a punch ball.

'Well how about we change just one opinion?' Joe said to me as though there had been no break in our conversation. Then before I could answer, he spoke directly to the young man: 'I'm not unemployed, and no-one's taking advantage of me. Come closer and learn.'

The young man started to laugh, but as Joe looked at him, the laughter died in his throat.

'Come closer,' Joe repeated, and much to my surprise, like a lamb, the young man came forward.

'Yes, your friends too. All come closer. Vic and I are going to change the world, and you've come just in time.'

So then, to my amazement, the friends, like an obedient flock, came over too.

'I'm confused, Joe,' I said. 'Are we changing the world or just one opinion?'

'Not sure,' he replied. 'It might turn out to be the same thing. Now let's hear about those crossroads.'

I looked about me and realized other people had joined the young man and his friends. There was a tiny, very elderly lady with one of those '50s retro shopping trolleys, only hers looked like it really *was* from the 1950s. There were also two young girls in what were probably chemist's uniforms, and a businessman in a suit who looked lost, as though he had wandered into the circle by mistake.

In the short space of time since the tattooed young man accosted me, we suddenly had an audience. Joe put his brushes down and un-crossed his legs. Everyone was looking at me.

'You know, Joe,' I said. 'I work in theater, but behind the scenes. I'm not used to center stage.' I tried to make light of it, but I was actually starting to get concerned. This was not what I had planned.

'It's ok,' he said. 'It's really just you and me.'

As he said that the other people seemed to recede. They were all still there. But it was as though they could not touch me, that I was under Joe's protection.

'Crossroads?' he prompted.

'I'm 48 years old,' I found myself telling him. 'I've had a lucky life. I have a job, I have a wife who loves me and I have a little money put aside. Not much, mind you, but a little.'

I looked behind me and saw the audience was still there, and for a moment lost my nerve.

'It's ok,' Joe told me, as though he could read my fears. 'No-one will embarrass or hurt you.'

It was like I was a little boy being re-assured. But that re-assurance felt good.

'I guess I just want to give back a little, that's all. I can go on designing another set, and another, and telling myself people like my sets, they get pleasure from them. And they do. I think they do anyway. But I want to do something more with my time, with the money I have.'

'There are lots of things you could do.'

I turned and saw it was the little old lady who had spoken. Her lips and her eyes were smiling at me.

'But that's just it!' I said, far more forcefully than I wanted. 'Wherever I look the problems of the world are so huge and my resources are so small, and it all feels so hopeless.'

I felt my head hang down. But whether I was bowing before the impossible, or just feeling embarrassed at my outburst, I didn't really know.

'Each according to his bounty,' Joe was saying. 'You give what you can.'

As I looked up he was smiling from ear to ear. It was as though he knew I was on the threshold of understanding.

'Let me tell you a story,' he said. 'We'll call it The Story of the Good American.'

'Is it like The Story of the Good Samaritan?' the Punchbowl boy was saying.

'A little like that,' Joe replied.

'That's a great story,' the young man enthused. 'Jesus told that story. You listen to the story, mate. Jesus was a great prophet. I'm telling you…'

But he was cut off by the little old lady, who, raising herself on her tiptoes, still looked about one third his size.

'You just be quiet now,' she told him.

And he was.

'This is a true story,' Joe continued. 'It's about a young man named Pete A. Vanderveer...'

'So you did work for him,' one of the chemist girls said. She obviously knew the rumors too.

Joe smiled at her: 'I didn't work *for* Pete. I worked *with* him.' Then his smile broadening, he said: 'In fact some might say he worked for me.'

'Is your name really Joe Stalin?' It was the man in the suit who had spoken. Perhaps he was less lost than he looked.

'My name is Joe," he smiled. 'The veracity of the surname can wait for another time.'

He was now silent for a moment. It seemed he was waiting to be sure he had everyone's attention.

'Pete was like you, Vic,' he said. 'He'd had a lucky life. Only his was luckier, or so the world would say. But of course it depends on your perspective. Cross-roads, big decisions, and perspective.' He smiled again. 'They're what make the world go round.'

2.

'It all began with Pete's father. Marcellus Vanderveer was a salesman for Random House. He worked out of Buffalo, where he lived with his family in a modest suburban home. But he was rarely at home. Marcellus was on the road all the time. He was dedicated and he was dogged. If he thought a book deserved to be a bestseller, he would make damn sure it *was* a bestseller, at least in upstate New York and Connecticut. There wasn't a bookseller in upstate New York or Connecticut who would dare say no to any book Marcellus wanted to sell them.

And he wasn't satisfied with just the initial sale. He'd be back in two weeks with "moved those ten copies of *The Life and Times of Margaret Thatcher* yet Fred?" And if Fred dared plead his customers in North Canaan Connecticut didn't really care about Margaret Thatcher, or perhaps didn't even know who she was, Marcellus wouldn't leave the shop till he had explained why it was essential that all 3000 residents of North Canaan, man, woman and child, possessed a copy of the book which would teach them all they needed to know about this remarkable woman.

So the bookseller knew he had a bare two weeks before Marcellus was back again, a bare two weeks to move those ten copies, if he wanted to avoid the wrath and the lecturing tongue of Marcellus Vanderveer. So he would corner his customers and by charm or discount, would move the ten copies.

But then of course Marcellus would say: "See, I told you they'd sell. This book is a winner. Here take another ten." By the time he had finished, North Canaan Connecticut would be the best informed town in North America on the burning question of 1980s British politics. Well, at least as informed as all the other towns on Marcellus Vanderveer's beat.

Back in New York City the executives at Random House would marvel yet again how Vanderveer had outsold the other salesmen ten to one, on a book they had taken under sufferance from their British subsidiary. And yet again they would offer Marcellus an executive position in head office.

But of course he refused. The man valued his freedom. He was not about to imprison himself in a life of commuting and high rise buildings. On the road his time was his own, and once he had tamed all the booksellers on his route, that time was abundant. And he used it to great effect.

He was, what you might call, an opportunist salesman, and he viewed a world where everything was for sale. Where others might see a broken down and rusty tractor, he saw an opportunity. In Mechanicville he would become a mechanic. He would get the tractor for peanuts, wheedle the aging spare parts out of someone for the price of a couple of beers and next thing you knew he'd be selling a spruced up machine for a spruced up price.

In Glens Falls he would pick up what had fallen off the back of Glen's truck, and would be selling it for a handsome profit down the road in Queensbury, where the profit he made would finance his next eclectic and creative deal.

All along he was building his warehouse on

the land he had at the back of his place in Buffalo, and stacking it with books. Out there he had a world of remaindered books he knew were only remaindered because the salesmen didn't have the talent to move them. From every part of the Northeast he gathered forgotten and neglected tomes for a song, or even just for the price of carting them away. By the late 1980s he had amassed hundreds of thousands of books and was selling them by mail order across America and beyond.

By the early 1990s he was starting to get rich. Amazingly he kept working for Random House. I think he didn't want to say good-bye to all those booksellers he loved to bully. Funnily enough whilst he was selling books on behalf of his employer, to the rural and suburban booksellers, in ones and twos and tens, he was selling books to the general public on his own behalf in the thousands.

He was a very busy man and he needed help. That was where I came in. I was young and was just starting to make a career for myself in the marketing department at Random House. But Marcellus plucked me out of there. I knew all about him of course. His reputation as a salesman was legendary. But I didn't think he knew I existed.

I was wrong. He knew all about me, where I'd trained, what I'd achieved, and he made up his mind he wanted me. He offered me twice what I was getting to be the marketing manager of *Never Ending Books Inc.*

Not long after that he did leave Random House. The business was growing at a rate even he hadn't predicted. It became 'our' baby. Of course the company belonged to Marcellus and I was just an employee. But it didn't feel like that. The man treated me like a partner, and it seemed like every other week my salary would go up. Then before I knew it the company had gone public and I was a major shareholder.

To say it was exhilarating was an understatement. In only a few years we already had a staff of several hundred. Then the internet happened and Marcellus didn't need to look twice to see the potential. He launched *Neverendingbooks.com*, which quickly morphed into *Neverending.com*, selling a never ending array of products.

The company became so diverse we started to hold 'what don't we sell?' meetings where all the executives would sit round trying to come up with something we had forgotten. It got harder and harder. But that for me was the best fun of all. Sometimes I would sit at that huge mahogany table in our Buffalo Office watching the brainstorming and trying to work out how I had got where I had got so quickly. But by the time I started to put the pieces together we were on to the next project. After a while it felt like there had been no beginning, as though it was what I had been doing all my life

In the meantime I had become part of the family. I was at the Vanderveers' most nights for dinner. I was included in most everything the Vanderveers did. That was nice because I was an only child and my parents had passed on.

Marjorie was a family doctor. She was a very smart and compassionate woman whose patients adored her. She looked on her husband's business interests with a mixture of admiration and amusement. She loved him very much, but seemed to have little interest in what he was doing, and equally little understanding of how it was all happening.

The money didn't mean much to her. She had her own income, and all those millions Marcellus talked about, just made her smile. She spent a lot of her time on charitable projects, both local and international. In Buffalo she was the one you called if you needed help. But she never asked Marcellus for money for any of her philanthropic ventures. Maybe she didn't think he would oblige. More likely she didn't feel it was her place. The money she needed she raised elsewhere.

They had one son, Pete, who was about my age. He was single and lived in a different part of town. Like me he would often dine at his parents' house. But he was very shy and although I would have said we were friends, really I didn't know much about him, apart from the superficial.

He had gone to Albany Law School and at one

point was Editor of the *Albany Law Review*. He was smart. Everyone acknowledged that. But his shyness was always going to hold him back. No-one doubted he had the brains to be a hot shot lawyer in New York City. But he just didn't have the right sort of personality, the right sort of ruthlessness, I guess. Besides it wasn't what he wanted. So he opened a small practice doing mainly property work in his home town of Buffalo.

Many were amazed how someone as outgoing as Marcellus could produce a son as shy as Pete. Some speculated Marcellus was too overpowering. But those who said that, didn't know the family. Marcellus loved his son with a passion but also with an intelligent understanding. He knew young men need to have their own space and their own freedoms. These he gave to his son, who, like Marjorie, made his own way in life.

What's more Pete adored his father. I would see the look on his face when Marcellus was describing his latest business coup. It was a look of amazement but it was also a look of admiration. He was not overwhelmed by his father but he did respect him, and he would have trusted him with his life. He sought his father's advice regularly, and that advice was like a sacred writ to Pete. Whatever Marcellus told him was the way he would go.

But soon Marcellus was about to offer Pete

advice he hadn't sought.

The news came out of nowhere as bad news is wont to do. Marcellus was a youthful 55 year old. He was fit and full of life. Now he had pancreatic cancer. As is so often the case with that disease, few early symptoms meant a late diagnosis. It had metastasized to the liver. Surgery was not an option. Marcellus was told he had very little time to put his affairs in order.

It was a cold Buffalo winter's day, about a week before Christmas, when Marcellus summoned us all to his study; Marjorie, Pete and me. The fire was roaring, and Marcellus was standing with his back to it. He held one typed sheet of paper in his left hand. It hung down by his side.

We had already known for a couple of days, but I think this was the first time the true horror hit us. Even before he spoke, Marjorie had tears in her eyes, and Pete and I were fighting them back too. There was something about that piece of paper which made everything, inexplicably, so real.

We all sat together on the couch in front of the fire, while Marcellus remained standing. He lifted the paper but only glanced briefly at it, before letting it slip down by his side again.

"I've made some notes," he said. "I'll give you all a copy later. But I wanted to say it to you first, say it out loud, because you are my family and you deserve more than a memo."

He sort of laughed then, and we sort of laughed too. But for me of course, it was so moving, how he had just included me as family, without even the merest qualification, and how Pete and Marjorie hadn't even noticed.

Then he turned to face the fire, screwed up the paper and threw it in. We all watched in silence as it burned away. We thought maybe he wouldn't hold it together. But we were wrong. When he turned back to face us he spoke gently and calmly. It was as though he had made a decision to retire early and wanted to spell out what the transitional arrangements might be. Just so there was no confusion. Just so we could get on with it while he went fishing. He spoke directly to Pete.

"I'm afraid it's up to you," he said, and his tone was truly apologetic. "There's too much riding on this; what we've created, what the market has come to depend on, all those employees."

There was a long silence then. We all knew it was the last thing Pete wanted. He had seen his father operate, and he knew he couldn't do life that way. I had no idea how Pete would respond. But it was Marjorie who broke the silence.

"I was hoping you'd offer me the job," she said, but we all knew there wasn't a skerric of truth in that.

"Would you really enjoy it?' he challenged her. "Even a little bit?"

"No," she admitted. "But nor would Pete."

"But…" he hesitated. "Pete has the toughness to pull it off. You don't."

There was silence again. Then finally Pete spoke:

"I'm not tough at all. Not at all." He hung his head, but whether from shame or just out of pure sadness, it was impossible to tell.

"You're wrong there," his father said. "You're shy. But don't confuse that with weakness. You have the resilience this company needs. You'll just look different from me. People will see you as aloof maybe, but maybe that's not such a bad thing."

"I know nothing of the business."

"That's where we are lucky," Marcellus said, turning to me. His eyes burned with a beseeching I will not forget any time soon. "We have Joe." It was the worst and the best moment of my life. "We do have you, don't we Joe? Pete has you?"

I looked across at Pete and not for the first time thought how little I actually knew this young man. He was tall, he was good looking, and he was always polite – these things I knew. But so did everyone. I knew nothing more of him than the rest of humanity. Still, I guessed I was going to have plenty of time to find out.

"Of course you have me," I told his father, who smiled his well-known smile, but said nothing more.

" I can't make you do it, Peter" he said. "But I'd be pretty happy if you did."

It was a remarkable understatement from a man who was about to die and as his dying wish was asking his son to change his whole life, give up his profession and take on a monumental responsibility.

Pete just looked at him for a moment, and then simply nodded his head.

"Thank you," Marcellus replied, after which there was a silence so long I started to get uncomfortable. Marcellus was waiting for something, but I didn't know what. Finally, ever so gently, he said to Marjorie: "There's just a few things I need to tell Pete now."

"Of course," she said, and got up to leave.

I got up to leave too. But Marcellus said:

"No stay, Joe. I want you to hear too. Just in case, if Peter forgets, you can remind him."

Marcellus now drew the armchair right up to the couch so the three of us were sitting in a conspiratorial triangle. He watched as Marjorie left the room, before beginning his brief but, as he saw it, essential course of instruction for his son.

"First of all, trust your instincts," he told his son.

"I don't think I have instincts," Pete replied in all sincerity. "I'm a lawyer. I have systems. I have logic. I don't know what instincts are."

"Well trust Joe's instincts, while you're waiting to recognize yours." Pete nodded and his father continued. "Then there will be all manner of people who want a piece of you. But say no.

25

Default to no. We give one million dollars a year to The Rockefeller Foundation. That's solid, that's generous. That's enough. Our obligation is to our shareholders and our customers. We're not here to save the world, are we Joe?"

"I guess not," I said.

"Then there will be business deals a plenty," Marcellus continued, "new deals, different deals. Deals with bells and feathers. But say no. Default to no. We have our business. It's one of the most varied in the world. More variety we don't need, do we Joe?"

"I wouldn't think so," I smiled.

I watched Marcellus talk, ever so earnestly to his son, and the voices disappeared for me. The mouths were moving but I couldn't hear them anymore. I became a silent voyeur on this tragically intimate moment between father and son. I think I had to switch out. It was the only way I could cope.

"Then there will be women," Marcellus was saying, as I came back into focus, "an endless stream of women. All beautiful, all loving you just for yourself. But it will never be true. If you choose to marry one, so be it, but know it will never be true, will it Joe?"

"It might be," I ventured, half-heartedly, trying to make a joke of what was clearly embarrassing Pete.

"There's no room for romance," Marcellus replied, totally seriously. "I wish you'd met someone while we were still poor. But you didn't. And you're going to get a lot richer than this. The chance of finding love is indirectly proportional to every extra dollar you earn."

"You don't make it sound like much fun," Pete told his father.

"I don't think it will be, for you," Marcellus replied. "That's why I feel so guilty about dying."

It was one of the strangest and saddest things I had ever heard, coming out of one of the strangest and saddest meetings I had ever attended. But Marcellus meant exactly what he said. His principal emotion, on facing death, was not fear. It was guilt. Guilt at leaving his son to finish a job, he, the father, had not prepared him for.

Then Marcellus rose, embraced his son, embraced me, and left the room. Not long after that he had left us altogether.

3.

Pete and I were both numb for a long time, throwing ourselves into the task Marcellus had set us, both for his sake and for our own.

Within three years we had tripled the number of employees, were working out of a head office at 42 Avenue of the Americas in New York City, and Pete had made the Bloomberg Billionaires' List.

That's the summary of what happened, the summary of what the world would have seen. But the personal side, for me, was something the world would never see, and most of it was far from anything I would have expected.

For the first couple of months Pete just sat at his father's big desk with the computer turned off and a note pad in front of him. His door was always open, and if you had watched him from the outer office you would have seen him staring into space a lot (thinking, one would assume), sometimes reading, and occasionally making a note on his pad.

From time to time his secretary would come in and let him know about a problem. He would just tell her to refer it to me. I would deal with it and then tell him what I'd done. He would always reply:

"That's fine, Joe. Thanks very much." And he would make a note on his pad.

Then occasionally I would have the sort of problem which, in the old days, I would never have tackled without first consulting Marcellus. So of course I did the same with Pete. Though soon enough I came to know what his answer would be.

"Whatever you think, will be fine."

So I would tell him what I proposed, and he would make a note on his pad, and smile at me. I would smile back and then leave his office, and go and do what I had intended to do all along.

The truth was I was running the company. I don't know how many people on the office floor understood that. Pete's secretary certainly did, and so did Marjorie, as it turned out. One day she came into my office with a bunch of flowers, so big she could hardly carry them.

"These are for you," she said, then smiled and turned to leave.

"Why?" I blustered.

"Because," she said, turning back to me, "I am very grateful."

"For what?"

"For what you are doing for Pete. For doing..." she was searching for a word, then just said: "For doing *everything*."

I was touched of course, by such thoughtfulness, in the midst of her grief. It also taught me that Marjorie knew exactly what was happening with the company, that she took a far keener interest in things than she let on.

When I thought about it I realized that of course she must. Of course she loved her son and had loved her husband. She didn't want to interfere in their work, but that didn't mean she didn't take an interest in what was central to their lives. And she was a smart woman. She would see immediately what was happening, where the problems lay.

In a strange way it gave me a greater sense of confidence in those early days. I felt if I came up against something really tough, I might just be able to go to Marjorie. It made me feel less alone. Although I never did go to her, that sense of a woman, a mother figure to confide in, would stay with me, and help me in a different way later on.

In the meantime I kept 'running the company'. Then one day, about three months after the death of Marcellus, Pete came into my office and invited me to have lunch with him. My secretary, who was in the room at the time, asked if she should book a restaurant.

"No need," Pete replied, smiling and producing two brown paper bags from behind his back. "Chicken sandwiches," he said. "It's a sunny day. Let's go to the park. You like chicken, Joe?"

So we sat in the park, side by side on a bench, and ate our chicken sandwiches. Pete obviously wanted to talk about something, but his shyness meant he was going to take a while to get round to it. Meantime we sat in uncomfortable silence. I wanted to say something, but for the life of me couldn't think what. Finally Pete reached inside his jacket pocket and pulled out a piece of paper. He passed it over to me. It was hand written, very neat, front and back.

"Tell me what you think," was all he said.

I started to read and realized it was a business plan. It was very concise and very logical. The narrative was on one side, the broad costings on the other. All there, on just one sheet of paper, was the destiny of our company for the next five years, as Pete saw it. It displayed a mature knowledge of what we did and a sensible approach to where he thought we should be going.

It even detailed a move to New York City within the next six months. But the thing that struck me most was an amount by way of tax deductible donation to a charity Marjorie chaired. It supported the training of eye doctors in the third world. The donation was to be $2 million per year.

"It's a great plan," I said.

"And Marjorie's charity?" he asked, as if reading my mind.

"Well, sure," I responded, tentatively. 'But Marcellus didn't think tax deductions beyond the Rockefeller were warranted, did he?"

"Marjorie didn't ask me," he replied, but not defensively, just as a matter of fact.

I thought it strange how he referred to his mother as Marjorie, when he was talking to me. I also thought it strange he had decided to dodge my question. But I let it pass. Hers was a great charity. No-one could object. And I sensed it was as much about Pete the son becoming Peter the CEO. And I had to admit it, was a nice way of making the transition.

Then slowly Pete started to take all the parts of the company into his own hands. One of his first acts after our picnic lunch, was the calling of a general meeting of all the employees. He hired out the ballroom at the Hilton Garden Inn, Buffalo Airport and catered a sit down meal for 300 people. I think the hotel must have got the wrong idea because all the chairs had those white chair covers with the big bows they have at weddings.

Everyone looked a little embarrassed and everyone felt a little out of place, myself included. Here we were at Buffalo Airport, in the grand ballroom, perched up on frou-frou white wedding chairs, waiting to see what the boss wanted of us. As it turned out he didn't seem to want much. Just to give us a good lunch, and more wine than would have been advisable. But as it was the boss who was doing the 'pouring', it didn't take long for most people to abandon their caution.

At noon, when we arrived, the only noise you could hear was the odd scraping of a frou-frou chair as someone tried to work themselves into a less uncomfortable position. By three o'clock the noise and the chatter, and in some cases the singing, were so loud you would swear we really were at the drunken end of a wedding.

Pete sat next to me and watched it all with satisfaction. Then around 3.15 he said:

"Joe, would you mind calling them to order?"

"Sure," I said, but failed totally to make myself heard over the noise. Even tinkling my spoon on a glass had no effect. It was only when I tinkled so hard it shattered all over Pete's secretary, and she screamed, that the audience realized their attention was required. Fortunately the secretary was unhurt.

Pete got to his feet to address the employees. I

was surprised. He was shy even talking to me, and here he was prepared to talk to the entire company. I've heard it said shy people are more comfortable with a crowd than an individual, because it is the intimacy they fear, and a crowd is never going to demand that of them. Whether or not that applied to Pete, he looked calm and in control.

"I'm sorry Marcellus has left us," he began, in a strong voice that immediately took control of the room. "He was a great man, and I loved him. I'm sorry too that I don't know any of you yet. But that will change. My door is always open." Then he turned to me sitting next to him: "Isn't it Joe?"

"It is," I said, not a little surprised.

"Any questions?" he asked, before there was any chance for applause. Not that I think anyone was intending to applaud. It just didn't seem appropriate somehow.

There was silence for a long time, until finally one woman from accounts payable tentatively raised her hand.

"Is the company really moving to New York City?" she ventured. "Because I couldn't do that. My kids go to school here and...". Her voice trailed off.

Pete looked genuinely concerned, and perhaps even a touch angry with himself for not realizing the rumor would have to get out, and would have to worry most people.

"Just head office, um..." he turned to me.

"Jenny," I said.

"Just the head office Jenny." His voice had a mellow kindness to it as he spoke. He was genuine. No-one could mistake that. "Everyone else will stay here. No job losses. Guaranteed." A tiny but audible sigh went round the room. "Besides we aren't going for six months. That gives me all the time I need to get to know you. And I'll be back lots. Promise."

Now everyone did applaud. There was a warm feeling amongst us all in the room that day. We had been treated to honesty, and refreshing brevity. We all appreciated it.

Whether or not he was comfortable making that brief speech, as I've said, Pete was definitely not comfortable one on one. Yet in the next few months, as he promised, he made it his business to meet, and get to know, every one of his employees. In my mind that took courage

Sometimes he would ask me to stay while he called an employee into his office. It was always awkward at first. That was never going to change. But in his own, deeply shy way, Pete had the common touch. The employee was always treated as an equal, and genuinely so.

Marcellus had played the democrat, but if you knew him, you knew he saw himself as the trailblazer, and his employees as the followers. His son on the other hand was a real democrat. He actually saw his staff as his peers. And they felt that immediately.

Marcellus too had always shown an interest in the lives and families of the employees, but whilst it was not insincere, it was charming and practiced, and had an end in view. Pete, on the other hand, genuinely wanted to know. This too his employees immediately understood.

Pete's father had been right about the number of people who had a deal to sell. But here again Pete surprised me. It would have been easy for him to set up a series of road blocks; secretaries, doormen, 'no-response' emails. But Pete wouldn't do that.

"You never know," he told me. "What if booksellers hadn't let Dad past the front door?"

So everyone with an idea had their moment in Pete's sun, or rather in my sun whilst Pete sat in the shadows. The way it worked was we would take them into the boardroom, and I would sit with them at the board table. I would hear the pitch and ask questions. Meanwhile Pete would sit in the back listening. For the most part, as Marcellus had recommended, he would default to no. But either way, like his employees, these people were treated with respect.

Then, as Marcellus had predicted, there was a world of beautiful women. He had said the chance of finding true love was inversely proportional to every extra dollar Pete earned. But what we came to learn was that the beauty of the women was in direct proportion to every extra dollar earned.

As Pete got richer the women got more

stunning. And somehow there was always at least one at every function or venue we went to, even when totally unexpected. We might, for example, be invited to one of Marjorie's charitable functions. The opening of a new wing of a clinic. The room would be populated with middle aged health professionals. But there was always one gorgeous woman who was just entranced with everything Pete had to say.

Admittedly it was hard work for them because Pete was shy and didn't say much. But he was always polite so, when accosted, would make some small talk, and the women would laugh uproariously and throw back their manes of glossy hair just to show how uproarious it was.

How they got there always remained a mystery. Pete of course never sought an explanation. He was too polite for that. But I sometimes did a little questioning. I wanted to know how a glossy haired young woman with a devastating décolletage had found herself amongst a group of middle aged gerontologists in ill-fitting suits.

But they were as slippery as they were beautiful. One stunning brunette, when confronted with why she was there midst the gerontologists, told me:

"You just need to have a feeling for the aged, a sense of their wisdom, and how the ravages of time have played upon their sense of self."

This of course was no kind of answer at all.

But that was all I was going to get, because she was straight back to Pete, and laughing at his latest 'witticism'.

He would always look across to me then, as if to say: "Was that really funny? Did I say something funny without realizing it?" And I would just shrug.

Marjorie once suggested there might be an agency somewhere, which kept tabs on rich men and sent their clients along to all the functions they attended. It wasn't such a silly idea. But true or not, I was just overwhelmed by their numbers. Like most young men growing up, I had personally seen very few extremely beautiful women, except in magazines.

Yet now they were everywhere, and I started to realize they were anything but a scarce commodity. I realized that whereas the average man might wait years to meet one really beautiful woman, a billionaire was going to meet one (maybe several) every day. This meant of course that by the simple laws of supply and demand, the billionaires had the upper hand. However the beautiful women didn't seem to understand that. Each seemed to think she was the only beautiful woman the billionaire had ever met. They all thought the simple act of offering themselves was all it would take. It was as if they had a unique commodity, let's call it sex for want of a more subtle word, and that commodity was theirs uniquely to bestow.

I recount all this not just as a second hand observer. I had the privilege, or was it the misfortune, to see it unfold at close quarters. As Pete got into the billionaire category, and the women got thicker on the ground, he found it harder and harder to cope. He was shy and he was honest, which is a terrible combination for dealing with predators. So one day he asked me for a special favor.

We were due to go to a civic function and he really wanted to talk to some of the key people. He didn't want to have to cut his way through the beauties first. At this point his face was not universally known. So he asked me if I wouldn't mind impersonating him for the night. I said that would be fine. I was intrigued to see what it felt like. So Pete lined up all the waiters and support staff to direct any young woman enquiring after Pete Vanderveer, to me.

I was very soon approached by probably the best looking woman yet. I'm sure my bottom lip hung permanently open, not just at her beauty, but because of her confidence and her charm. She stayed at my side all evening just making me feel like the greatest guy who ever lived. After a while I started to get a little guilty. This was all fun in theory, but here was this lovely young woman who didn't deserve to be deceived, and I wasn't going to do it any longer.

"Look," I said to her at last, "I've got to tell you I'm not Pete. I know it's terrible, but Pete wanted some privacy tonight, and I agreed to be his double, if you know what I mean, that is..." and my voice just trailed off. I felt totally stupid.

She had just been watching me with those big eyes of hers.

"That's all right, um. What is your real name?"

"Joe. I'm Joe," I mumbled, feeling more ludicrous all the time.

"That's all right, Joe," she said. "Don't feel bad. I understand." And she placed her lovely white hand on my arm for a blissful second. "So who is the real Pete?" she smiled.

Naively I pointed him out. She smiled again, and left me. Within seconds she was chatting to Pete, laughing and touching him on the arm, just as she had done with me. I can't really describe how I felt then. But the word 'forsaken' keeps coming to mind.

After that I needed to be pretty drunk before I would agree to impersonate my boss. As for Pete, he remained calm and polite with all of them. Sometimes he would take them up on their offers, but he never shared any of those details with me.

Of course he gained the reputation of being a playboy, and the magazines and tabloid press voted him one of the most eligible bachelors in America. It really was ridiculous because he spent most of his time trying to avoid the women. But it would only take one to slip through the net, entwine her arm in his at a gathering, stare into his eyes at a cocktail party, and there would be a photographer, waiting to snap the 'happy couple'. Marjorie thought the photographers were sent along by the same agencies that sent the beauties. They came as a package deal.

Sometimes I would come into Pete's office and he would be reading one of the tabloid stories with a wry smile on his face. He seemed to take it all in his stride. Yet he was a lonely man. Marcellus had told him there was no hope of finding a woman who was genuine. He had pretty much accepted his father's judgment, and from what we had seen, he was wise to do so. And there is never such loneliness as when there is no hope.

Nonetheless when it came to the company I was surprised to see, very pleasantly surprised to see, that Pete Vanderveer *had* found something to love. Maybe love is too strong a word. But he had found something to get his teeth into, and now that challenge was starting to bring him out of himself.

The shy provincial lawyer, though still shy, was becoming the 'can do' businessman. The man who didn't want the job, who was sure he couldn't do the job, was relishing it every bit as much as his father had. What's more he had taken the legacy Marcellus had left him, and grown it to a powerhouse perhaps even Marcellus would not have expected. But soon that powerhouse would be using its energy in a very different way.

4.

Sri Lanka was in the middle of a brutal civil war. But that didn't stop Marjorie. She was there with her charity to train eye doctors.

"That's where they need us the most," she said.

The rural poor of Sri Lanka, as in so many parts of the third world, were suffering from eye diseases which sent them blind. Yet most were treatable and usually reversible. The cost of surgery, once the doctors were trained, could be as little as $25 dollars a time. Eyesight could be restored for a pittance. It meant Pete's $2 million dollars could save the sight of 80,000 people a year.

The problem in Sri Lanka was that the fighting was everywhere. No corner of that little country they called 'The Buddha's Tear' was safe. So getting into the villages could be very difficult, and for the doctors and nurses, very dangerous.

But Marjorie was not going to let her own safety stand in the way, and she found a team of people just as courageous. So Pete's cure was being delivered to places no-one thought it could get. The medical profession of that ravaged country was grateful. They, unlike their politicians, drew no distinction between Tamil and Sinhalese. They wanted to thank Pete. They were determined to have a lunch in his honor. But Pete was shy and particularly troubled by public displays of gratitude. So he sent me instead.

I had a few days in Colombo before the lunch, a kind of brief holiday it was supposed to be. I don't know what I was thinking. Who holidays in a war zone? But an elderly Sri Lankan friend in New York told me not to worry. He said the dangers from the civil war were overstated. He said I would find a beautiful, welcoming country. Well he was suffering from either nostalgia or Alzheimer's.

The noise and the madness of the traffic, the heat and the dust, were unbearable. The machine gun wielding guards on every street corner, often stood forlornly and redundantly guarding a pile of rubble that once was a building. As for 'welcoming', I'd met nothing but anger and frustration from customs officials to cab drivers to less than helpful hotel clerks. The poverty was palpable and the beggars clung like lethargic flies.

At first I tried to give money to all of them, but more than once the beggar would turn out to be a professional trickster; a legless man who had tucked his legs under his garment, a deaf mute who called out to his friend moments after getting money from me. My worst memory was a young teenage boy carrying the limp body of his little brother over his shoulder. When I gave them money the little brother came to life, jumped off the shoulder, they both blew raspberries at me and ran off laughing.

So then I became cynical and wouldn't give to anyone, which was just as silly as trying to give to everyone. There were so many in real need. But how to tell the difference? How to know where to give and where to hold back?

I was thinking about this as I drove down the Galle Rd to the lunch. It was to be at the Southern tip of Colombo, at the famed Mount Lavinia Beach Hotel, on the sea. I watched the surging mass of humanity as the driver of my 'limousine' as they called it, my hot rattly little hire car, would crawl through the traffic, beggars scratching at the rolled up windows. Then he would speed off narrowly missing the people darting amongst the cars with a world of different goods on their heads.

I was thinking about all I had seen and experienced. But my thoughts could form no pattern. All I knew was that Marjorie didn't have a problem working out what to do with her bounty. She was doing good work for people whom she knew needed it. Perhaps it was because she took her destiny into her own hands, made firm decisions about where she could and could not help, and followed through with that.

Maybe I could too, if I stayed longer. But I didn't want to do that. This place was hateful and I wanted to get out. I didn't want to think any more about who was and who wasn't deserving of my charity. I just wanted to get back to New York. But first I had the lunch to attend.

Initial impressions of the Mount Lavinia Beach Hotel were not promising. The premier resort in the capital was badly in need of a paint job. I don't think it had been bombed, but it might as well have, for all the bits of masonry and electrical wiring that hung loose, looking like macabre Christmas decorations. I was greeted by a doorman whose uniform had obviously been borrowed from a man twice his size, and probably had never seen an iron, nor indeed even a laundry.

The dining room too was dilapidated and ill lit. The tablecloths yearned for a clean as much as the doorman's livery. Nonetheless I was greeted by the President of the medical body, Dr. Senanayake, as though I were a demi-god. His attentiveness and his excessive flattery were polar opposites of what I had experienced so far. In fact they were so extreme I felt just as uncomfortable as I had all week, but obviously for quite different reasons.

"Mr. Starling! Mr. Starling!" he exclaimed again and again, as he almost waltzed me around the room to meet everyone. "Mr. Starling! Mr. Starling! Respected representative of the esteemed *Neverending.com*. Dr. Weeraratna, have you met the esteemed Mr. Starling? Dr. Fernandez, this is our wonderful Mr. Starling? O my goodness." And he would waggle his head in that well known subcontinental way, that looks like a 'no' to westerners, but means something like 'yes' and/or 'of course' and/or 'o my goodness'.

Occasionally I would catch sight of Marjorie out of the corner of my eye, but had no chance to even say hello. For her part she seemed quite amused by my predicament. Eventually, when all introductions were finally and mercifully over, Dr. Senanayake seated me next to her at the head table.

"You look a little overwhelmed," she smiled.

But before I could answer, Dr. Senanayake had launched into his speech of welcome and gratitude to *Neverending.com* and to me. I don't remember much of what he said, but it built on the enthusiasm he had shown whilst introducing me round the room. His speech was quite long. So I had a little time to settle down and recover from the turmoil of the last week. I had time to reflect.

I realized that more than twenty years of civil war had driven this country into extreme conflict, poverty and despair. That extremism was going to reflect itself in everything the people did, from the way they 'earned a living' in the streets, to Dr. Senanayake's desperate desire to keep me on side and make sure Pete's money kept coming through. It was understandable. I determined then I would try to be more sanguine, more relaxed. I would accept these people on their own terms.

But as an astute Australian ex-patriot journalist once said: "In a war zone it's never wise to relax. The next big surprise is just around the corner".

I was about to discover the wisdom of his remark. What's more it would be another Australian who would spring the first surprise. After Dr. Senanayake's speech I made a speech in reply and then took questions from the floor. Most were polite, and more in the form of expressions of gratitude, than real questions. But then a young woman stood up.

"Katherine Matheson," she announced, and on some level my mind acknowledged her Australian accent. But though I knew she was now talking, and obviously at some length, I couldn't focus on what she was saying. This woman had hit me between the eyes, between the ribs and amidst the loins, and very quickly too, it seemed. It was not something I had ever experienced. I was conscious of feeling silly and confused, because I couldn't work it out.

It all happened very fast of course, but in those few seconds I managed to acknowledge that she was very beautiful, with long wavy dark hair, pale skin and a slim willowy body, all of which made her look like she had just stepped off a tarot card.

But the way she looked couldn't possibly be it. Over the past few years I had met so many beautiful women, the whole concept had lost its bite. Maybe it was the way she spoke, with a strange mixture of humility and confrontation. But then how did I even know that? I hadn't heard most of what she'd said. I'd just picked up tone and body language and the odd word about money and courage and a hungry world.

I didn't have time to take my musing any further. Now Dr Senanayake was on his feet and signaling her to finish up.

"I don't think that is quite fair to Mr. Starling. After all he is merely an emissary for his company, which has been extraordinarily generous…"

"That's not the point," the woman began, interrupting him quite sharply. But a hum of disapproval from the crowd stopped her saying anything more. She sat down, looking at least flustered, perhaps angry, I wasn't sure.

I began to realize I was in a very embarrassing position. I couldn't possibly answer her question for the very good reason I hadn't heard what she said. However I couldn't tell her I hadn't heard, and certainly not why I hadn't heard. Now, because of Senanayake's interruption, I had the option to simply ignore her question, but I didn't want to do that either. My heart went out to her. That was not something I could control right now. I wanted to help. To make her feel better. In the end I said:

"I have to apologize. I was confused by Ms. Matheson's question. Perhaps you could repeat it, Ms. Matheson".

She got slowly to her feet and looked at me disbelievingly.

"Are you making fun of me?" she said. "I would have though what I said was clear enough."

"Nonetheless," I said, apologetically, turning to Margie for support, but finding only a confused shrug, "If you could just summarize...", my voice trailed off. I was feeling not a little uncomfortable, and quite foolish.

"All right," she said. She was not angry. She spoke quite gently and in a measured tone. "I will summarize, if I can. I understand Mr. Starling is just an emissary, and I understand *Neverending.com* is giving $2 million dollars per year to this cause, but *Neverending.com* has a turnover of many billions of dollars per year. Two million dollars is a tiny fraction of its profit."

She paused for a moment to look at me, and in that second I thought she understood what I was feeling. I still don't know if that were true. But she certainly softened her tone even further.

"They could give more. That's all I'm saying. If *Neverending.com,* and all the companies like it, gave what they really could afford, world poverty and unnecessary disease would end. That's all I'm saying."

She sat down and I kept looking at her. For far too long I suspect. Then I heard myself say:

"Do you really think that's true?"

"Which part?" she asked.

"About the end of disease and poverty."

"Yes," she said, her voice still soft, but determined. "It's a simple matter of arithmetic. Divide the total cost of curing poverty and disease by the revenue of the world's biggest companies, and those companies are still left with a healthy profit. Healthy enough to keep all their shareholders rich and ensure the company's continued survival. What's more, by saving all those lives and alleviating all that poverty, they've just got themselves a whole new market."

There was absolute silence in the room, till finally Dr. Senanayake said:

"That's nonsense. That can't be right."

"How do you know all that?" I asked.

"I've done the sums," she said. "I can show you some day if you'd like."

I wanted to say: "Oh yes please, show me now. Any reason to be alone with you." But of course I didn't, and the debate was in effect closed by Marjorie who stood up and said:

"I'm sure your sums are right, Katherine. But my late husband had some firm views on charitable spending, and my son has gone way beyond what he promised his father. What he is doing is wonderful. I can't ask him for more. You mustn't either."

"Yes of course," Katherine said, quite simply.

And so we moved to a few more questions, and then to mingling afterwards. I tried to get the chance to speak to Katherine alone. But something or someone always got in the way, till I finally lost sight of her and assumed she had left.

"Who is she?" I asked Marjorie when we had a moment together.

"An Aussie lawyer, or was. Got disillusioned and came over here looking to help. Gives us free legal advice from time to time. Does work for a lot of other charities too."

As the function started to wind down, I decided to take myself for a walk along the beach right next to the hotel. I took my shoes off and shuffled through the soft sand at the back of the beach just below a park. Down by the water's edge young men were laughing and swimming and their women were paddling in the shallows, their saris hitched only a few modest inches above the ankle.

The late afternoon sun was very hot and the sparkle from the water was blinding. It was perhaps a vision of the beautiful, welcoming Sri Lanka my New York friend had spoken of. I was feeling a mixture of emotions right then. Despite Dr. Senanayake's over attentiveness, I had been touched by the whole proceeding, and was feeling glad Pete had sent me, which was far from what I had been feeling a few hours before.

Then of course I couldn't get Katherine out of my mind. I still had no way of describing to myself the emotions she had stirred in me, and I kept thinking about what she had said. Whilst it didn't diminish Pete and Marjorie's achievements, I couldn't help seeing things in another light now.

It was a lot to take in and, as I kicked at the white sand, my mind was far away from the place where I found myself. Maybe that's why it took me so long to realize what was happening.

There was a pinging sound near me, and then another. But what was it and what was making it? Suddenly things seemed to speed up. There was yelling down by the water's edge and both men and women were diving into the shallows or head first into the sand. Behind me in the park people were running in all direction. Their screaming made no sense to me.

Even when I looked again at the shoreline, now deserted of locals, and saw four men, two kneeling, two standing, all with rifles to their shoulders; even then my mind refused to tell me what I needed to know.

Then from what seemed like just near my left shoulder gun fire began. At last I knew what it was. And it was very close. Men in the park, uniformed, obviously Sri Lankan army, were firing down on what must have been Tamil rebels on the shoreline.

Now my mind understood, but as another bullet pinged into the rocks only feet from me, it refused to give my body the instructions it needed. Here I was caught in the cross-fire of a gun battle, and I was just standing there. It might have been only a matter of seconds since the first shot rang out, but they were all seconds too many.

Then just as I felt myself slowly turn I was hit with a thudding tackle. Someone had thrown their body at me and driven me down into the soft sand. Her face was on top of mine. My face was half covered in her hair, half buried in the sand. I could smell perfume.

My first thought was: "Maybe this is Katherine. I hope this is Katherine." Here I was, as close to death as anyone could possibly be, and all I could think about was Katherine. Not worried about survival, not curious about what to do next. Just hopeful the woman who had saved my life, was Katherine. And what were the chances of that?

"When I get off you," she yelled in my ear above the din, "crawl very low toward the hotel. Don't lift your head. They don't want to shoot us, but those Tamils have some very old and very unreliable weapons."

All I could think then was: "Is that an Australian accent?" Still no reflection on what she had just said, on how dangerous this all might be. Only thought - is she yelling at me in an Aussie voice?

Then she had climbed off me and I was crawling through the sand. She was crawling behind me, shielding me. We were getting away. The gun fight was going on. But all I could think was: "It *is* Katherine. I think it really is." And even though the gunfight hadn't got my heart beating, this thought did.

I turned back to look at her, and my heart skipped for a second because it was, it actually was her.

"Keep going!" she screamed at me.

5.

That night I was still shaken. What I had been through would be with me for a while yet. But I was feeling a little calmer. I'd had a couple of drinks, and I was having dinner with Katherine.

In the short space of time since she had come into my life, she had made quite an impact on me, and in more ways than one. Part of that impact was a sore rib cage.

"Any rugby fullback would have been proud of that tackle," I said.

"You were a sitting duck," she laughed. "Next time sprint for the corner, and watch me take you into touch."

"When the occasion arises, I'll look forward to it. But stationary target or not, your technique was impeccable."

"I had three brothers who played for the Galloping Greens. You had to learn to tackle if you wanted to preserve anything you owned."

"You preserved my life," I told her. My tone sounded far too serious. I had had a few drinks, and deep down must have been trying to communicate how I felt about her. But it didn't come out right.

We were silent for a few seconds.

"I played for Randwick too," I told her, and as I spoke recalled her surname was Matheson. "In fact," I hastened to add, "I played with your brother George. We were on opposite wings."

"You played for the Greens?"

"Sure did," I beamed with pride.

My rugby career had been brief and unmemorable. But now it seemed like my greatest gift. Because of course I was looking for any way to impress her, any way to deepen the contact. Nonetheless I knew I had to reign it in. There must be no silly statements, no drunken declarations, I tried to tell myself.

She seemed to like me, but when you've shared a confused debate about billionaires and charities, and then a lifesaving adventure, it would be hard not to like someone. If I were honest, I would have to admit, I saw nothing beyond that.

"Still you did actually save my life." This time I managed to lighten my tone. "I would like to do something for you, something to express my gratitude."

"Don't be silly," she said. "I would have done it for any ex-player." Then she stopped and thought for a minute. "Left wing? George was on the right, you were left? Skinny kid, bad haircut?"

"Yes. That was me."

"You weren't much chop."

"I haven't heard that expression in a long time."

"Make you feel nostalgic?"

"Not really. Not when it so cuttingly sums up my rugby career."

"No, that's not fair of me," she smiled. "I saw you score a try once."

"It was disallowed," I said.

"How do you know which one I'm talking about?"

"Because…". I waited for her to get it.

"Because there *was only* one," she burst out laughing.

"Exactly."

"No, not really."

"Really." I hung my head in mock shame. ' "So you see, after letting the team down, and then stumbling into a gun fight so you had to risk your life to save mine, I would feel much better if I could do something for you."

"You could make a donation to my favorite charity," she smiled.

"Which one?"

"No I was joking. Just referring to what a pain in the ass I was this afternoon."

"You weren't," I rushed to assure her. "What you said was interesting. And passionate. I like that." I could feel myself sliding towards a risky declaration, so quickly added, as soberly as I could: "Seriously it would give me pleasure. Which charity?"

She looked at me for a moment, and for that brief second I dared to think I saw a spark there for me. But in the end I decided it wasn't real. Still, one day, maybe. Have patience, I told myself.

"That would be nice," she conceded

graciously. "It's up in Kotaheña, right in the heart of the slums. It's called The Good Sisters Home for the Dying. Three or four very overworked nuns look after about a hundred dying people."

"What are they dying from?" I asked.

"It's officially and euphemistically known as Hansen's Disease."

If I hadn't been so infatuated with her I would have asked why it needed a euphemism. But at that moment I didn't care what sort of disease it was. If she liked it I wanted to like it too.

"Would a million be ok?" I heard myself saying.

"Dollars or rupees?" she laughed.

"Dollars of course. Well actually it would have to be for $999,999. I have authority to write cheques for *less* than a million dollars."

She looked at me, not sure if I were joking.

"I'm not joking," I assured her. "I can do it."

"I'm sure you can," she said, now quite seriously. "But I don't want you to."

"You sing a different tune from this afternoon."

"That was a whole other situation," she insisted

"Why? Because it was theory, and this is reality."

I wasn't sure if I had stepped beyond what was safe, both for our new friendship, and anything else I might hope for. She was silent for a couple of moments. I could see her thinking, weighing up factors in her mind. Finally she said:

"No strings attached?"

Had she guessed? Up to this point I had been telling myself my motives for offering her the money were pure. Because they were – at least in part. Did she suspect my true feelings or was she talking more generally? It was impossible to tell, and it would have been incredibly tasteless, not to say self-destructive, to ask.

"No strings of any kind." I told her firmly.

"Then you are a wonderful man, if not a such a good rugby player, and I gratefully accept. The nuns will gratefully accept too, I'm sure."

It felt wonderful to be called wonderful by her.

"What will they do with the money?" I asked.

"I don't honestly know," she confessed. "They've never had a donation like that. Mostly it's a few rupees for some bed linen, or some bandaging. But I know they won't waste it."

I saw she was becoming very embarrassed, as though, having accepted, she now needed to justify.

"Why did you leave Australia?" I asked to change the subject.

She seemed glad I had.

"I tried the corporate lawyer gig in Sydney," she said, "but the power suits pinched the life out of me."

"You would look good in a power suit," I smiled. She looked at me a moment, and I hastened to say: "I mean you would handle the power suit very well, I'm sure."

"Not really. I was a shy kid…"

"No-one would have guessed this afternoon."

"Well I was. The boardroom scene taught me to talk, taught me to look confident. But deep down I was always shy." She stopped for a minute. "And I found it all so soulless. I'd gone into the law to do some good, but in Phillip St that looked like naivety – in the extreme."

"So you gave it away and came here?"

"First I tried working for Aboriginal Legal Aid in the Territory."

"In Darwin?"

"In Alice, and the settlements and missions round about."

"That must have been different."

"Different…yes. Out on the settlements, it's as far from Sydney as anywhere in the world."

"You didn't like that?"

"I liked the people. They have a wisdom about them that comes from taking your time, thinking before you speak. When I was with them I didn't feel shy. Like me they looked shy. But they weren't because they didn't fear intimacy. So I stopped fearing it too. I stopped being shy"

I didn't quite follow her, but it occurred to me I might send Pete out there.

"Sounds good," I said.

"Yes but there was nothing I could do for them. Two hundred years of white settlement with all its greed and disease and dislocation and just basic genocide, needs to be solved by politicians and social workers and teachers. When a young aboriginal man commits a crime because he's just so angry, as a lawyer you can achieve one of two things. You can *fail* to keep him out of jail which only helps to make him angrier, only helps to perfect his criminal skills. Or you can *keep* him out of jail which only delays the problem. When one of my colleagues said 'This is like treating cancer with a band-aid', I knew it was time to go."

"So then you came here?"

"Here, India, Nigeria. Wherever people like Marjorie are doing such amazing work."

"You could have stayed in the Red Centre. Fred Hollows does just what Marjorie is doing, for the same people you were trying to help."

"It sounds silly," she said, "but if I stayed in Australia I would always have felt like a lawyer. I needed to leave Oz before I could be something else."

This was something I understood. As a Maroubra boy whose parents just wanted him to get a good apprenticeship, I had needed to get away too.

We talked for a long time that night about what we had done with our lives. I kept looking for a sign from her, but no amount of alcohol seemed to bring it on. At least I didn't think so. Only time might do that, time and opportunity. And I didn't know what opportunities I could find. I had to go back to New York. I wasn't sure I would be able to return to Sri Lanka. I wasn't sure I could find an excuse to get her to the US.

When we parted that night she already had her cheque. We shook hands. She said:

"Thank you again, Joe Starling."

I laughed and she looked confused.

"It's just that I had forgotten - when an Australian says my name it sounds more like Stalin than Starling," I explained. "Perhaps I'll change it to Stalin one day, just for fun."

"Joe Stalin," she laughed. "It shouldn't suit you, but maybe it does."

6.

Back in New York I had a problem. My largess with Katherine had been a little misplaced. Sure I had authority to write a big cheque. But that depended on an unspoken trust. I was trusted to write cheques for company business. Marcellus had been very clear what that might include. Pete had stretched the envelope, but beyond that he had been equally clear.

How would Pete take it? Would he brush it aside? Would he be angry? Might he even accuse me of fraud? I thought he would probably be ok, but I couldn't be sure. In any event what I should have done was go straight to tell him. What I should *not* have done was wait six months till the auditors picked up the expense as being 'extraordinary and outside the business plan'.

I sat in Pete's office like a naughty schoolboy whilst he paced up and down trying to think how to tell me what he had decided to tell me. I felt for him. For a man with his temperament this was very hard.

"What I don't understand is how this woman got to you."

"She got to me because she saved my life. That will do it every time." I tried to make a joke of it, but that was never going to work.

"Couldn't you have bought her a bunch of flowers with a thank you card?" He was still pacing. Then suddenly he stopped. "You're in love with her aren't you? That's it. You've fallen for this Aussie crusader."

He was standing side on to me when he said that, and looked at me out of the corner of his eye. It made the accusation so much more damning.

What I should have said was: "Of course not. Don't be ridiculous!" Instead I hesitated. That is a dead giveaway for any witness under cross-examination, as he well knew. Then after what was probably only a few seconds, but felt like a lifetime, I finally said:

"That's completely irrelevant." And in so saying I dragged the arrow of accusation fair into my own heart.

Pete just sighed and slumped down in his

office chair. He swiveled about for a minute, finally coming to rest leaning back on the chair's hinge as far from me as he could get.

"You know it qualifies as embezzlement."

"Don't be ridiculous. Do you really care about one million dollars?"

"I don't," he said. "But we have shareholders. They care about every dollar."

"Well don't tell the shareholders."

Pete looked at me for longer than he had ever looked at me before. I thought I saw the beginnings of a tear in the corner of his eye.

"I love you like a brother," he said. "No, that's not true. I love you more than I could ever love a brother. I owe you…"

He couldn't finish, and now the tear did emerge and ran down his cheek.

I wanted to rush over and hug him, but we had never touched. It just wasn't how we did things. Marcellus had been an old-world, firm hand shaking, man's man. He had passed that on to Pete. No hugging and back slapping for us. So I just sat there feeling about as silly as I had ever felt, and impotent to arrest Pete's distress.

"You can fix this," I eventually said, as gently as I could manage. "You could ratify it retrospectively."

"Maybe I could," he said, with infinite sadness in his voice. "But maybe I don't want to. My father made it very clear how he wanted us to run this company. I know I fiddled with things, gave the annuity to Marjorie's charity. But, Joe, this is my company. I can do that. You can't. Maybe if you had come to me, straight away. But you deceived me. That's what I can't get past. It shows you weren't comfortable with what you'd done."

"I guess that's true," I said. "So what do you plan? To have me arrested?"

"Don't be crazy."

"Are you sacking me? I agree I'm not much chop."

"What's that mean?"

"Sorry, I was thinking back. Just an Australianism. Are you firing me?"

"You're way too valuable, as you know. I have a much better idea." He brushed the tear from his eye. He had a plan of action. I could tell by the way the sadness disappeared and the focus returned. This is what he had been working up to tell me all along. "We're going to get the money back," he said. "Best idea, don't you think?"

I couldn't imagine how we would do that, but was in no position to argue.

"Guess so," I said, letting out a long sigh. "OK I'll get over there this week and see what I can do."

"Oh no, you'd like that, wouldn't you?" For the first time in this long tense interview Pete had the semblance of a smile. "You'd like to get back to your great love. Well forget it. I'll go myself. I assume we can find her. I assume you're still in contact with…"

"Katherine. Yes we have exchanged the odd email."

"Made the odd call?" he prompted, now breaking into a full blooded smile.

"Yes," I said, "just the odd call. But Pete, I want you to know she is not my great love." I hesitated for a minute. "At least as far as she is concerned."

"She doesn't know how you feel?"

"I guess not."

"Ah." He got up and paced about some more. Finally he stopped and turned to me. "In that case you better come too. I'll get the money. You get the girl."

7.

We had arranged to meet Katherine at the Pagoda Tea Rooms at 10 am, but by 11.30 she still hadn't shown up. Pete was angry. I was sad.

When I had told her why we were coming, it may have been the most embarrassing moment of my life. It would have been hard enough in person. But on the phone from 9000 miles away, with the awkward silences, it was excruciating. The big man who had made the big donation now had to ask for it back. I think I apologized around 75 times.

But she had been understanding, even compassionate. She had agreed to do what she could to recover the money, and was happy to meet with Pete. So her not showing up didn't make sense. Nonetheless after we had tried more varieties of Dilmah tea than was prudent, it was clear we were wasting our time.

"We had better do this on our own," he said, standing, reaching into his pockets and throwing a stack of rupees on the table. It was as close as I had ever seen Pete get to an act of overt frustration. "Do you know what the place is called?"

For the life of me I couldn't remember, which meant Pete had to ring our chief accountant and get him out of bed at 2 am. Fortunately he had a note of the 'extraordinary payment' in his briefcase at home. So we avoided him having to go down to the office. That was a blessing, I guess. But however you looked at it, this day was not starting well.

"The Good Sisters Home for the Dying," Pete told the cab driver.

"In Kotaheña?" he asked.

Pete looked at me. I could see the frustration level hitting the red zone.

"Is there more than one Good Sisters Home for the Dying?" I asked the driver.

"No just one," he said, waggling his head vigorously, which can also mean 'obviously' or 'why would you ask?'.

It was a slow hot trip and we had plenty of time to take in the increasing squalor as we got closer to the slums of Kotaheña. Eventually we passed by a tumbled down Portuguese style church and immediately after swung hard right, at top speed, through a wide opening in a dilapidated once white stucco wall. The taxi driver was forced to screech to a halt to miss two children who raced across in front of the car.

The car skidded in the mud. It flew everywhere including over the two children. But that didn't seem to bother them. In fact they ran off laughing, and having taken their cue from the cab driver, picked up more globs of mud and hurled them at one another.

We paid the driver, disembarked into the ankle deep mire, and then were spattered with mud as the cab sped off. Unfortunately Pete was wearing mainly white. It probably didn't help his mood. I refrained from trying to wipe him clean, fearing I might just exacerbate matters. He tried to wipe himself but of course succeeded only in smearing the mud more evenly over all his clothes. I did the same with mine just to be friendly.

When we had finished our futile cleaning attempts I realized we were on the edge of a cricket match. A child about 10 years old was batting in front of a garbage bin wicket on a makeshift pitch that was so makeshift it wasn't any different from the rest of the field. In other words, the wet season had given them a mud pitch in the middle of a mud field.

Another child around his age was bowling to him with something that looked like balled up socks. He had to bowl every ball as a full-toss because of course the socks wouldn't bounce much, even on a hard surface, let alone in the mud. The bowler and batsman were surrounded not by the standard 10 fielders but by a screaming mob of probably 50. They were all incredibly skinny and incredibly loud. They were packed into a space that would barely qualify as an infield.

"What are they doing?" Pete asked.

"It's a cricket match," I told him.

"Really? It doesn't look like cricket. Is that a cricket bat?"

"Probably a fence post. But that's how they do it in the subcontinent. Out of that melee of cricket madness will come the next Mahela Jayawardene."

"Who's he?"

"He's a batsman and next in line to Shiva. They're crazy for the game here."

"Here in the Home for the Dying?" he screamed over the din of the players.

"No I meant here in Sri Lanka. But it is strange they're allowed to play in the grounds of a Hospice. That noise can't be good for the patients."

I went over to one of the outfielders, though he wasn't much further from the bat than the infielders. It was one big mass of screaming fielders really. He was an older boy of perhaps twelve years.

"Excuse me," I yelled, "why are you playing cricket here?"

He looked at me for a moment and it occurred to me he didn't speak English. But then he said, waggling his head, (which can also mean 'I don't understand' and/or 'I'm sorry'):

"Is it troubling you, sir?"

"No I love cricket. I'm just wondering why you are playing *here*."

"Well of course because we live here."

"All of you?"

"Yes, sir, every last one of us."

Obviously I was not looking forward to relaying this last piece of intelligence to Pete, but then I couldn't really hide the fact.

"I think the cab driver has brought us to the wrong place. These kids live here."

The day was getting worse. But to Pete's credit he held himself together. Nonetheless he took my arm a little too forcefully, as he led me back to the same boy.'

"Is this a school?" he asked.

"No indeed, sir," the boy waggled, for the waggle of the head can also mean 'no indeed sir.' "This is an orphanage. We are all orphans, don't you know."

Pete turned to me for a moment. He said nothing, but he didn't have to. His eyes said it all.

"We are looking for The Good Sisters Home

for The Dying," he told the boy, who, brightening at the possibility of being of help, said:

"Then you are in luck, sir, for you are in that very place, right now."

"I thought you said it was an orphanage," Pete sighed, wilting under the inscrutability of the Orient.

"Yes indeed, it is both. The Good Sisters Home for the Dying, and the unofficial Good Sisters home for the orphans."

At that point we walked away from the melee to try to find some quiet and some shade. About 100 yards away there was a once white stucco building with a wooden awning that did give a little shade. We sheltered there for the moment, trying to make some sense of it all. Then my phone rang.

It was Katherine. Apparently an elephant had sat on her car the day before in Kandy. Her phone had been trapped in the car under the elephant, and when she had recovered it, realized phones were not elephant proof. That's why she hadn't been able to call. But she was on her way and would meet us at the Home for the Dying. I tried to explain our confusion, but she just said not to worry, we were in the right place. It was all very complicated, and we should just hold on till she got there.

"No wonder she suckered you," Pete grinned. "An elephant sat on my phone. The woman clearly has a gift."

Just then the door opened behind us and a wrinkled, deeply tanned old nun came out. She looked about 80. She was not Tamil nor Sinhalese. She didn't seem surprised to see us.

"You must be Joe and Pete," she said. "Welcome. Welcome to you both. Now which is which?"

Her voice didn't seem to fit the weathered face. It was young and full of bounce. Her English was flawless, but she had an accent I couldn't place.

"This is Pete," I said. "I am Joe."

She took my hand and kissed it. Then she did the same to Pete.

"I am Sister Assumpta," she said. "The Lord blesses you. You are lodged deep within His heart."

It was pretty clear Katherine hadn't told her why we were there. As if reading my thoughts Pete said:

"I take it Miss Matheson hasn't told you why we are here."

"Oh yes," the nun replied quite calmly, smiling at us. "You want to get your million dollars back."

"And that makes you happy?" I couldn't help asking. Nothing was quite adding up.

"Yes because you *can't* get it back," she said, still maintaining a remarkable equanimity. "We have spent your money. We have built a beautiful new hospital. The money is all gone." She paused for a moment and then, no doubt seeing our stunned looks, repeated: "On the hospital. On building the hospital. It's a lay down mazaire."

"A what?" Clearly Pete could feel himself drifting further from reality every minute.

"It's just an expression from *Five Hundred*. An Aussie card game."

Even then it took me a couple of moments to realize.

"Your accent! I couldn't place it but you're an Aussie!"

"Collingwood via Ballarat," she smiled. 'Dorothy O'Reilly, of the Ballarat O'Reillys."

I felt I should say something like: "Oh, the Ballarat O'Reillys. Well what do you know?" But I just smiled. For his part Pete said:

"Unbelievable! You're everywhere. Are there any of you left in Australia?"

"I don't know," she said. "I've been away for 50 years. They might all be gone by now." She laughed a tiny laugh. "That's why you couldn't pick my accent. After Collingwood there was Calcutta and Goa before here. But let's not stand in the sun any longer. Let's go in for a refreshing drink."

She ushered us into the building we had been standing near. Inside it was darker and cooler, for there were only two tiny windows placed very high up the rough stone walls. The floor was made of stone too. At least the floor had been made of stone once upon a time. Now it was a mixture of broken stone and sand.

She asked us to sit down, but when Pete went to sit on a wooden bench just inside the door, she rushed over to stop him. He was almost half way down when she grabbed him under the armpits, showing quite remarkable strength in getting him back on his feet.

"I'm so sorry," she said. "That bench is only for the children. The legs are very wobbly. A full grown adult will smash it to tinder."

She showed, very briefly, what I thought was a cheeky grin.

Once Pete and I had been settled on a safer wooden bench, another much younger nun entered with an unopened carton of coca cola. She carefully opened it, produced two plastic bottles, and handed them to Pete and me. But the nuns did not take one for themselves. The bottles were of course warm, and so anything but refreshing. But we could see they were precious cargo, reserved for special guests.

Neither of us were coke drinkers let alone warm coke drinkers, but we sipped slowly for fear of offending. As we sat silently drinking our cokes, Pete would look across at me as if to say: "Why am I worried about offending this woman?" Yet he sipped on in silence. It was clear no business would be done till we have swallowed all 375 ml of the warm sickly-sweet substance. Eventually Pete threw back the last third and said:

"Sister, I just have to ask. If you know we

want our money back, why did you kiss our hands and tell us God loves us?"

"Because you *gave* us the money." She said, quite simply. Seeing that we still didn't understand, she added: "When you did that your hearts were pure and full of charity. I understand how corporations work. Shareholders put pressure on you. Your own Board puts pressure on you. Eventually you give in. But you held off for over six months, which gave us time to build.

"God was making sure the money would be used as you yourselves had originally wanted it to be used," she continued. "Here in the Third World we learn that Our Lord is a practical God. He likes results. The details along the way don't matter much. I kissed your hands because you are great men who did a wonderful thing. We have a very practical and very useful hospital. After that, who cares?"

She gave us a huge warm smile then, as did the younger nun.

I wasn't sure whether I should try to set her straight. On the one hand honesty compelled a confession that I, and I alone, had given the money, but with a slightly tainted motive, and without authority. On the other hand I wasn't sure if Pete wanted her to know that maybe God didn't quite see him as a 'great man who did a wonderful thing'.

In the end I didn't have to decide because just then Katherine appeared in the doorway accompanied by Marjorie.

"Mom, what are you doing here?" Pete said.

"Katherine asked me to drive her. An elephant sat on her car."

They both went to sit on the bench near the door.

"Don't sit there!" Pete yelled, causing them to spring up again.

"It's fine," said Sister Assumpta. "The bench is quite secure." Then she gave one of her tiny laughs. "Just my little joke."

Katherine and Marjorie looked confused. Pete looked unimpressed, to say the least.

"It's just the Aussie sense of humor," I whispered, trying to mollify him. "It can be a bit weird sometimes."

"More Irish than Aussie," said Sister Assumpta, obviously having overheard us. "My father was such a joker. He played tricks like that all the time."

"And you've carried on the tradition, taking it half way round the world," I said.

"I have indeed," said Sister Assumpta proudly, her eyes twinkling. "I have indeed."

I had been looking across at Katherine the whole time. There was a part of me hoped she wouldn't make me feel the way she did, anymore. But it was not to be. If anything the surge of emotions was even stronger, the proverbial absence no doubt having made the heart grow fonder.

But, worse still, she wasn't looking at me. She was looking at Pete. In fact her eyes were staying on him all the time. For his part, Pete had yet to really notice her, what with the wooden bench joke and Sister Assumpta's Irish heritage stories. But now I saw him look across at her, and my heart sank somewhere near my shoelaces, because his eyes were staying on her too.

How long could they stare at each other? Did anyone else notice? I looked across at Marjorie, then at the two nuns. But no, it was my privilege alone. I wasn't sure whether I wanted to run away or just cry. However I wasn't given time to do either. I watched as Pete did all but twist his head with his hands to drag his gaze away from Katherine.

"Sister Assumpta," he said, his tone unmistakably official, "there have been some unfortunate misunderstandings here. But the fact remains we want our money back. If you can't give it back, or are unwilling to do so, we will have no alternative but to take the necessary action."

"Are you going to sue us?" Sister Assumpta smiled, her tone so light by comparison to Pete's.

"Your order, or the builders, or both."

Sister Assumpta nodded to herself for a moment.

"Do me a favor," she said. "Come and have a look at the hospital. We are very proud of it"

"It won't do any good."

"Please," she smiled again. "If you are going to bankrupt us, at least you can indulge me first."

Pete looked around. Marjorie was looking imploringly at him, Katherine was smiling. What could he do but agree?

We walked out into the humid air again, and past the cricket match which was still being contested as vigorously as before. I was up front with Marjorie and Sister Assumpta. Pete and Katherine were together behind us. They had obviously introduced themselves. Once we left the noise of the cricket match behind, I could already hear them chatting like old friends and even laughing together. What was there to laugh about? Weren't we threatening to sue them?

I felt like the Phantom of the Opera, sad, ugly and lustful. Like him too I was vengeful at the sound of the beautiful young couple exchanging their love talk. If that sounds a trifle dramatic, for me it was dramatic. The world would have noticed nothing. But when you want something so much for yourself, as I did, you notice every nuance which is telling you that you are not going to get it, that someone else may get it instead.

After a time, having walked past a number of old, dilapidated buildings that were not only in the Portuguese style, but looked like they may have been built by the Portuguese before they left in 1650, we turned a corner and beheld the new hospital.

Its sparkling white newness stood in contrast

to all that had come before. It could have been the new wing of the Royal North Shore in Sydney, only much much smaller. In fact its size was the first thing Pete mentioned.

"Is this all there is?" he asked the nun.

"Don't you like it?"

"It's fine. That's not the point. How many rooms? How many beds?"

"We have four wards, each with 30 beds," she said proudly.

Pete started walking around it then, and we all followed till he had done a complete circuit. Then he strode into the front door and made a quick circuit of the wards. We all continued to follow along behind. Back at the front door he said:

"Did you give all the money to the builders?"

"Yes," said Sister Assumpta. "Almost."

"How did you negotiate the price?"

"We didn't have to negotiate", she explained. "They asked how much money we had from our benefactor. We told them we had one million dollars. They said how wonderful that was because luckily the hospital would only cost $950,000, leaving us a whole $50,000 for linen and bandages. That's a lifetime of linen and bandages."

"Is this another one of your Irish jokes?" Pete said, a little too forcefully.

This time Sister Assumpta didn't give her tiny laugh. Nor did she even smile, but hung her head.

"It's not an Irish joke," she said.

I could see Pete was instantly ashamed of himself and so spoke much more gently to her.

"The thing is, Sister, this could be built for half a million dollars in New York. Here with cheaper labor, it would be a lot less. You've been cheated, and very badly."

"I see," she said, still hanging her head. But she was not one to dwell on the negative for too long. She soon raised herself up, and essaying the faintest smile, said: "But still, we have the hospital, and it is so wonderful. Please come and have a look. You just rushed through the wards. Come and meet some of our patients. Please. Come and see all our clean new sheets and pillow cases and our clean new bandages."

So we set off on a proper tour of the hospital. The other nuns who worked there emerged from the wards to join us, and we made quite an official party. Sister Assumpta took us from ward to ward and introduced us to several of the patients, all of whom expressed their gratitude to Pete and me. One old woman said:

"Gentlemen, you have made my last years a pleasure."

Pleasure. It seemed such an incongruous word to use. I was moved by the courage of the woman. I was amazed too, what a difference a little comfort can make.

It didn't take us long to notice that although the patients were all of different ages, they had the same obvious external symptoms; skin lesions, sometimes very severe, sometimes causing extreme disfigurement of the face. And because the heat had them lying on top of the bed, we could also often see tissue loss from their fingers and toes.

We noticed, as well, on the floor under each bed were one or two straw mattresses.

After the second ward, Pete turned to Sister Assumpta:

"These people are suffering from leprosy, are they not?"

"Yes of course," she replied. "You didn't know that?"

Pete turned to me. I told him I didn't know. I turned to Katherine.

"I thought you understood," she said. "I thought that's why you were so keen to give, because it is such a worthy cause."

"You told me they were suffering from Hansen's disease."

"That *is* leprosy," Marjorie said.

"I said they were suffering from what is *euphemistically* called Hansen's Disease," Katherine added, looking bewildered. "I thought you knew what I meant. I thought you knew that was leprosy."

"I didn't." Now it was my turn to hang my head.

Pete walked away from us for a moment down the central corridor. We all looked at one another, but no-one spoke, until finally Sister Assumpta said:

"What does it matter what you thought, Joe. It *is* a worthy cause."

When Pete came back, he said to Marjorie:

"I thought leprosy was curable these days."

"It is," she said. "In fact since '95 the World Health Organization, together with the pharmaceutical companies, have been making some drugs available to endemic countries for free."

"Then why don't these people have the drugs?" His question was half to Marjorie, half to Sister Assumpta. Marjorie answered:

"For all the usual third world reasons. Mismanagement means a lot doesn't get beyond Government stores, and when it does, corruption means it has a price on it anyway, that only the handful of wealthy sufferers can afford. Then even if there is no corruption, there is the war which makes it hard to get the medicines where they are needed. Beyond that there is the barrier of superstition. Leprosy has a stigma, sometimes being seen as a curse from above. People don't want to go near the sufferers."

"But it's not very contagious, is it?"

"Not very."

"And these sisters aren't worried by the stigma. They are working with the sick. Why don't they have the drugs?"

"Miscommunication and misinformation," she

said, "and, pardon me Sister, but just plain ignorance."

"Did you not know about the drugs?" Katherine asked the nun.

"We had heard something, but most of our patients are Tamil. People here say it is a Government trick to kill them."

Everyone, all at once, let out a sigh of disbelief.

"Do you believe that?" Pete demanded. "You are an educated woman."

"I'm not as educated as you think. I went to an overcrowded convent school for girls in Ballarat, and left at the age of 15 to enter the order. I haven't read a book in 50 years." Pete started to speak, but she held up her hand. "No, I don't think it is a government plot. The Sinhalese Government has done some terrible things over the years, but I think if they really wanted to kill off the Tamil lepers in Kotaheña, they would find a much more efficient way." Pete went to interrupt again, but once more she held up her hand. "I *have* tried to get the drugs from the Government, if you must know. I have had a dozen meetings at a dozen different Government departments. They all smile and make promises, but six years on nothing has arrived."

We all went quiet again. I could see Pete was thinking. I was aware too Katherine was watching him think. After a while he said to Marjorie:

"How do the drugs work?"

"Leprosy is caused by a bacteria," she explained. "There's a more serious multibacillary form and a less serious one. They both respond to antibiotics. The antibiotics come in monthly multi-drug blister packs. For the multibacillary you need 24 months' worth and for the less serious 6 months' worth."

"How much does it cost?" he asked.

"I'm not sure exactly," Marjorie said, "but a 24 month course is maybe $40, or $50 at the most. For the 6 months' course, around $10."

Pete shook his head, then asked the nun:

"How many people here have the worse form?"

"I didn't even know there were two forms," the nun confessed.

"You can't tell without a test," Marjorie explained. "Sister Assumpta would never need to know the difference. Everyone would die in the end. Her only concern is to look after them while they're living."

"It's crazy," Pete mumbled to himself as he walked away down the corridor again.

We all watched him down the other end. It was like he was debating with himself. When he returned Katherine was asking Sister Assumpta:

"Why are there mats under the beds?"

"For the children to sleep on," she said quite simply.

"The children sleep under the beds of the lepers?" Pete spluttered as he came back into the group.

"Of course," the nun responded. "Where else would we put them? The sick people must have the beds. Now it is all so clean for everyone, even on the floor."

"I just don't understand," Pete said. "Why run a home for lepers and an orphanage at the same time?"

"It is not a choice, Mr Vanderveer," she said, for the first time becoming emotional. "The church asks us to run a home for the dying. Then the war makes orphans. They turn up at our door. If we don't take them they will die. What are we to do? Send them away? Say 'We are sorry children, this is a home for the dying, so now you have to die elsewhere'. I know we are risking their lives putting them so close to the sick people. But it's a chance we have to take. There is no chance for them outside these walls."

Marjorie had tears in her eyes.

"It's all right Sister," she said. "We understand."

"Yes," Pete said after a long silence. "We understand." He turned to Marjorie. "Let's assume they all have the worse form of the disease. There are about 100 people here. It would cost around $4000-5000 to cure them all. Correct?"

"Correct."

"So we have spent one million dollars to build a hospital for people to die in, when we could have cured those same people for no more than

$5000?"

"I guess that is correct too," Marjorie replied.

"Mom, you must have known all this."

"Yes of course, I have come here with Katherine several times."

"Why didn't you tell me? I could have helped."

"My darling boy," she said. "Why would I tell you? Your father was very clear, and you have been generous beyond anything he would have approved. We are saving the sight of 80,000 people per year thanks to you." She paused for a minute, as she was at risk of becoming emotional herself. She so loved her son. She admired everything he did. She didn't like him being in this position. "And what would you have me tell you?" she said after a time. "That you could save the lives of 100 people in Kotaheña for just $5000? Why would I mention this place out of all the places I could mention? In every pocket of this country there are people who are dying unnecessarily, from a range of treatable diseases, where the treatment costs next to nothing by western standards. Why would I choose this one to tell you about, out of the thousands of examples I could choose?"

Pete looked at her like a child who has suddenly understood something in the adult world.

"Sister Assumpta," he said, "if I buy the drugs for these people, and my mother is willing to organize it…"

"I'll organize it," Katherine insisted.

"Very well, if Katherine organizes it, will you be happy to administer the drugs to these people until they are well? And as each one recovers and leaves, can you promise me you will eventually convert the wards to dormitories for the children to sleep in?"

"I was not wrong when I said God holds you in his heart, and I would love to do as you say. But the children will have to stay under the beds I'm afraid."

"Why?" Pete was shaking his head in disbelief.

"Because whenever a leper dies, there is another waiting outside the gate to be let in. Whenever a child grows strong enough to make it on the streets, another child is waiting to take her place."

"Once they know there is a cure here, there will be a line of lepers stretching from Kotaheña to Jaffna," Katherine said. "The only way you will ever turn this into an orphanage, is if you cure every leper in Sri Lanka."

After a very long silence Pete asked her in all seriousness:

"Can I do that?"

"Of course you can. You're the only one who can." Her answer sounded so natural. It was as though she had been waiting for that very question. Then she told him how and why:

"The Sri Lankan Government are never going to do it, because they are incompetent or corrupt or superstitious or just don't care. They say they'll do it to keep the World Health Organization happy. But the will is not there. Some first world governments have said they'll do it, but they never will because they fear losing votes if they spend too much money on overseas aid. So the World Health Organization tries to do it themselves. But they have to rely on the Sri Lankan Government to implement it. So we are back to where we started.

"But a billionaire like you can do it. You're rich because you're smart and efficient. When you say you'll do something, you will, because you have no other agenda. Once you have made your decision it is a simple matter of logistics."

"I wouldn't say simple," Marjorie smiled.

"Ok but no harder than building a company the size of *Neverending.com*."

"A lot easier than that," Marjorie said.

"How many lepers are there?" Pete asked.

Katherine looked at Marjorie. "I've heard around 20,000?"

"In a war zone with thousands of remote villagers, it's impossible to tell," Marjorie said. "It could be a lot higher."

"And of course there are new cases all the time," Katherine added.

"Let's just go with 20,000 for the moment," Pete said. "We want to keep things simple for the accountants. They're always so much happier when things are simple, aren't they Joe?" He turned to me and smiled.

"I've always found 'less is more' with the accountants," I said.

"I'll get a discount buying in bulk, won't I?" Pete asked Marjorie.

"I'm sure the drug companies are open to a deal."

Pete did a quick mental calculation.

"Probably cost us less than $400,000."

"Double that," Marjorie said. "By the time you employ people to go into the towns and villages and take into account other unforseens, like some of those people being shot."

"It's still cheaper than what we spent to build this hospital."

"Do I take it you are discontinuing your legal action?" Sister Assumpta gave her little laugh.

"I'd like to nail those thieving builders," Pete said. "But I think we need to concentrate our resources, look to the future. Wouldn't you agree Katherine?"

"I would," she said, giving him a smile I would have given my life to receive.

"Will you do it?" he asked her. "Will you run it for me?"

"You bet," she said, without a moment's hesitation.

8.

On the way back in the plane, we sat together in silence. There was an unacknowledged presence, perched on the console between our business class seats. After two glasses of wine I turned to Pete and said:

"Well I guess you showed *her* who's boss!" It broke the ice. I could see the beginnings of a smile in the corner of his mouth. But he said nothing. So I added: "What I don't understand is how this woman got to you."

I was of course throwing his own words back at him; when he had scolded me, before we left for Sri Lanka. His smile got broader, but still he didn't feel the need to speak. So I said:

"I recall we went to Colombo with two aims, to get the money back and to get me the girl. As we achieved neither of those, would you say our trip was a total failure?"

"Judged by the original agenda, I'd have to say yes."

"But now there is a new agenda?"

"I think there is." Pete turned to me, suddenly looking quite serious. "I'm sorry you didn't get the girl, Joe. I really am. But maybe someday."

"You don't believe that," I said.

"I guess I don't," he confessed, a sadness creeping into his voice. Whilst his words didn't help me, his tone, strangely enough, made me feel better. I guess it was being reminded my happiness mattered to him.

"So what is the new agenda?" I asked.

"It seems we are now in the 'Let's Cure Sri Lanka of leprosy' business."

"Not much doubt about it," I said.

"It bothers me, Joe, to be honest. I made a promise to my dying father. Rockefeller and no more. Then it was Marjorie's eye doctors, and now this."

"Most people's opinions are molded by what they've seen," I said. "It limits them. Marcellus saw a world of books and a world of business. If he'd seen what we saw, there in Colombo, he would have done exactly the same."

"Do you really think so?" His voice was almost imploring. "Nonetheless, I did make a promise."

"Do you read the bible as a literal document?" I asked.

"No," he said, looking at me quizzically.

"Marcellus was your bible for business," I told him, "and in many ways for life. But he was never meant to be taken literally."

It was like I had removed a load from his shoulders. He seemed to straighten as he sat there, lift himself up, almost.

"Thanks, Joe," he said, and I knew from the way he said those two simple words, that I had given him a gift.

But Katherine's presence was still there. We had not dealt with everything. It was in Pete's nature to be able to leave the rest alone. But it was not in mine.

"We went to get me the girl," I said. "But I think we got her for you."

I expected a strenuous denial. But that's not what I got. Instead he said, again with a certain sadness in his voice:

"I can't trust them, Joe. You know I never will. That part of Marcellus' bible will always be with me."

"She's got to be different," I found myself saying. "She's not the usual aspiring actress or escapee from the model agency. This is a woman who has given up material things, to risk her life in the Third World."

I couldn't believe I was arguing her case, his case, their case. But my friend Pete was really the best friend I had, and I couldn't not do it.

"Even so," he said, "for the time being I have to leave things on a business basis. Marjorie says she will do a great job with the leprosy. I'll support her…"

"The odd email, the odd call," I gently mocked.

"Just the odd one," he smiled.

So there it was. Pete and Katherine could be a reality. Katherine and Joe could not. Whether he felt as I did, whether his feelings ran as deep, was not something I could question him about. We may have been good friends, but there was a conversational line we could not cross. This was on the other side of that line.

Back in New York Pete seemed perpetually restless and I was pretty sure I knew why. I was suffering from my own restlessness. We were restless twins. Two men yearning for the same woman, both prevented from acting on their emotions, but for very different reasons. Sadly, my reason was solid, whilst his was a fabrication of the mind. But of course it was not my place to tell him that.

Marjorie, however, was free to speak. One day, about three months after our return, she took her chance at the end of a Board meeting when the three of us were alone:

"I think Katherine is doing a good job," she said.

Pete nodded, but didn't look at his mother.

"I thought she would," I ventured.

"But, you know, Pete," she added, "it's a big job. She's a smart woman, and dedicated. Still, I know she'd value a visit from you. A little face to face help and advice. Even just some moral support."

"Do you really think that would be valuable?" he asked, still not looking at his mother.

"Oh, undoubtedly," she pressed.

Well, I think it took Pete about seven minutes to be on a plane to Colombo. And about seven minutes after that Marjorie was in my office.

"I had to do it, Joe," she said, a look in her eyes that begged for forgiveness.

A part of me wanted to pretend I had no idea what she was talking about. But that would have been an insult to both of us. So I just said:

"You love him. You want him to be happy."

"I do. I so want him to be happy."

"There's a barrier to get past," I ventured.

"She'll get him past it," was all Marjorie said. Even then I knew she was right.

9.

"The problem is," Pete was telling me, "you can't just give money and walk away." I told him I understood. But he kept explaining. He needed to convince himself. "Imagine if we decided to invest in a new business, but just handed over cash to a group of people we didn't know, and hoped they got it right. We'd be crazy, wouldn't we?"

"We'd never do that," I agreed.

"Even if you put someone you trust in charge."

"Like Katherine."

"Yes like Katherine. She's clever and hardworking, but what does she know about business?"

"Not much, I guess."

"Precisely. And it's a business, Joe. The

business of curing leprosy is a business, like any other. If you don't treat it that way you won't succeed."

"Agreed."

He looked at me then, as though realizing for the first time I was in the room.

"That's why I need to be in Sri Lanka so much."

Almost 18 months had passed since the leprosy project had been launched, and as time went by, Pete was going out to Colombo more and more. He was right of course. If it were going to work, the project needed Pete or someone like Pete to be there on the ground. But of course there was another reason. I thought it was time we stopped dancing about it.

"You could send me," I said. "I could do it just as well." It was a challenge to him - to come clean. He didn't know how to answer, because of course there was no answer, on the official version. So I also said: "You also want to be with Katherine."

He looked at me for a moment as though he genuinely never expected me to raise the subject.

"I do, Joe," he said at last. "I admit it. But you know we're just friends, and colleagues of course. Nothing has happened. Absolutely nothing."

That actually surprised me.

"Then she's a very patient woman," I couldn't help laughing, "and you have a problem you need to solve."

We were in Pete's office. He sat down heavily

in the big old swivel chair, and it creaked and sighed, as though burdened by the weight of that problem.

"I actually have two problems," he said, "my inability to trust, and my fear of betraying you."

Again he had surprised me. It was a forthrightness I was not accustomed to.

"The first problem," I said, "well, you have to work that out for yourself. But as for betraying me, I can tell you, for sure, that is not possible."

"Have you got over her?" he asked like a hopeful little boy.

I wanted to lie to him, but in the end all I could manage was a semi-lie:

"I'm moving in that direction," I said. "Anyway I'm your friend. You have my total support."

Any objective observer would have seen a problem in the way I answered. But Pete was not objective. So it was the green light he was hoping for. He looked about him as though he didn't know how to respond. In the end he said:

"One problem down then."

"One to go," I smiled.

"But you know what, Joe?" It was the little boy again.

"What?"

He hesitated for a moment, as though assessing whether it was safe to speak. Then suddenly he just burst forth, a big smile on his face.

"I really love it," he almost sang. "Nothing has ever made me so happy. When I was a lawyer I thought I wanted to be a lawyer, but really I was all bound up. I was so shy I could barely tolerate myself, and I was achieving nothing. Then you and Dad gave me the gift of the company, and suddenly I had something to do that felt real, that felt right. But it's nothing compared to the work I'm doing out there. The incidence of the disease is decreasing. The infection rate is dropping. The death rate has halved. People are alive thanks to us."

I had never seen Pete so enthusiastic, nor so open. More importantly I had never seen him speak with such fluency. It was like the work gave tongue to itself.

"And I don't feel shy anymore." He continued. "Not at all. When I'm out there I feel I can say whatever I want, to whoever I want. I don't know why that would be. But my fears have retreated along with the retreat of that terrible disease."

It was quite amazing to hear him talk that way. We had all known, always, what a terrible disease Pete's shyness had been for him. But none of us ever dreamed of broaching the subject.

"Katherine may have had a part to play in that," I ventured.

He thought for a moment and then said:

"I really don't think that's it. Not the way you mean it. Sure I love being with her. And she is like me. She once was lost but now is found." He gave a tiny laugh. It was the sound of pure joy. Then he said: "But for me, like her, the healing comes from doing what you know you are meant to do. That's what takes away the fear."

10.

Within a short space of time Pete was out of the country pretty much full time, and I was *de facto* running the company again. Over the next twelve to eighteen months the charitable works of *Neverending.com* expanded as fast as the original business had done. Marjorie's charity and the leprosy program were now operating outside Sri Lanka in India, Bangladesh and parts of Africa. Pete had also made moves to set up programs for agricultural development on the subcontinent and in the Horn of Africa.

Ever since he had taken over the company he had been a man who got things done, but now his energy level was like never before. He was propelled by a joy which touched everyone around him. So I was happy to look after the business side of things. I felt I was doing my part too.

There was never a moment we didn't get support from the other shareholders. Pete, Marjorie and I held the majority of shares and could have done what we liked. But Pete wanted to make sure everyone was on board. So early on he called an extraordinary meeting of shareholders, and told them what he had told me. As with me he was totally fluent and perfectly frank. It was as though he were a different man. Not one single shareholder opposed the direction he was taking.

Of course Pete understood just how much he was relying on me and he wasn't going to take it for granted. One day he came back from Colombo, went straight from the airport to his office, and before even his secretary was allowed to bring him up to date, he called me in.

"I'm not going to let you do all this for nothing," he said.

"All what?" I smiled. It was fun to play coy.

"I'll stay on as Chairman of the Board. But I want to make you CEO," he said. "You are anyway. This will make it official. Plus there will be more money and shares."

"I don't actually need the title or more money. I'm rich enough. For a working class Bra Boy this is enough."

"A what boy?"

"It's not important."

"No, tell me."

"A Bra Boy is a boy from Marou*bra*. It's the beach suburb where I was born. We were lifeguards. We were supposed to be tough. We were proud of our working class origins. CEO means nothing. It's the Bra Boy title that counts."

It felt like a clumsy way to reject a generous offer. But Pete didn't seem to take it that way, though he did look confused.

"I see," he said at length, though he clearly didn't. Then returning to the subject at hand. "Do it for me. If you accept all the baubles, I'll feel a lot less guilty."

A wise man once said the greatest gift you can give is to receive, gracefully. So I accepted Pete's generous offer and became the world's richest Bra Boy. But then he had some other news for me, which was going to be a little harder to accept, with grace.

"We're getting married." I heard him say. Then he added: "Katherine and I." As though there could be any doubt. "And we're going to set up a foundation. It will be called the *Pete A. and Katherine Vanderveer Foundation*. We'll run it together. It will make everything we're doing so much easier, so much better from a financial, not to mention a tax point of view."

"More importantly it will give you the right sort of profile, to attract others to what you're doing," I heard myself saying.

"You're right!" Pete said, his voice so full of gratitude and enthusiasm. He had obviously worried about how I was going to take the news.

Of course if he had been able to see inside my head he may not have been quite so comfortable. Inside my head was a tumble of thoughts. My body too ached with a dozen conflicting emotions. I was happy for Pete. I was happy for Katherine too. I might even say I was happy for the world, because they were going to make a formidable team. They already were. But of course, for me, it was the closing of a last door which I didn't even know I had been trying to keep open.

This complex of thoughts and emotions, I needed to work out over the next days and weeks. For the moment I just said:

"So you got past the second problem?'

"She got me past it."

"Marjorie said she would. How did she do it, if I may ask?"

Pete blushed at my question, then said:

"*She* proposed to *me*."

"Simple as that, was it?"

"Not quite," he said, his blush receding a little. "She said that her proposal was conditional on my signing a pre-nup agreement..."

"Really?" I said. I was surprised. This didn't seem to fit.

"...where if we separate she is to get nothing."

"She gave you a foolproof way to trust," I heard myself say.

"She did," he said, with a mixture of pride and delight.

The wedding was scheduled for a few months hence. It was to be a small family occasion in Central Park. In the meantime I got on with being the new CEO of *Neverending.com*. But along with the title and the job, life in general had suddenly got harder, because now I was wrestling with how I would handle seeing Katherine again.

There were times I convinced myself it would all be fine. Sure she would be as beautiful as ever, I had no doubt. Sure she would excite me like she always had. But I was a grown up, and just enough time had passed.

But then I would have a dream where I was running screaming from Central Park, having lost all control and sense of decorum, expounding my misery to the joggers, railing at the drivers of the carriages about the unfairness of life. I would stop at the sight of lovers embracing on the grass, and scream at them to stop it and just go home.

Then I would wake and all my good intentions would have been flushed away. It would take me the rest of the day recover. And so I oscillated for a few months until the day arrived.

I can't say I remember much about it. Perhaps like the accident victim who goes into shock, I was protecting myself by fading out. I think we were in the Conservatory Garden, and I think the celebrant was a middle aged woman with unusually large teeth. I know it was sunny because the sun had a tendency to glint off those teeth. I'm pretty sure I was best man, though what I did or what I said, I have no idea. And beyond that the details are lost to me.

I do remember, in my anaesthetized state, Katherine was lovelier than I had imagined. I felt certain too, as I looked at her, and she looked back at me, she had no idea how I felt. Nothing I had done in our brief times together had alerted her. For that I was glad. But of course it also filled me with a deep sadness bordering on emptiness.

The ceremony had been in the morning. Now Pete and Katherine were going to spend some time alone before the small afternoon reception at The Plaza. As our family group separated, I think Marjorie asked me how I was. I don't know what I answered, but suddenly I was alone walking down 5th Avenue beside the Park. I was still in my dreamlike state. But now a determination was coming upon me, a consciousness that I would not yet have been able to put into words. Nonetheless I knew what I was going to do, more or less. And certainly I knew I could never go to the reception.

I went back to the office, and called in our chief accountant Stanley. Stan had been the one who kindly got out of bed at 2 am to tell us we needed to go to the Good Sisters Home for the Dying. When he came into my office and sat on the other side of my desk, he had a strange expression on his face. It may just have been a reaction to the strange expression I no doubt had on mine.

Anyway I started to give Stan instructions, and to his credit he did not once interrupt me or question what I was doing. Maybe my expression was daunting, maybe disturbing, or maybe Stan was just a good company man who did what he was told.

"So Stan, first draw out $10,000 in cash. From my personal account mind you, not the company account. Then I want you to prepare a deed of gift for me. Get legal to help if necessary. I want it back on my desk by 3pm. Sorry to rush you, but that's how it has to be. In the deed of gift I will give all my shares in the company and all my personal savings and other assets to the *Pete A. and Katherine Vanderveer Foundation*. I'll be here at 3pm to get the cash and sign the deed."

He nodded. Then stayed seated for a moment in case there was more. But clearly my face told him there was not, because he suddenly jumped to his feet and was gone. While he was away I used the time to cut up my credit cards and write my letter of resignation. I composed and discarded several long tortured drafts before realizing I had to keep it simple. Nothing was ever going to explain what I was doing, not to anyone's satisfaction, not if I penned a hundred page exegesis on the inner workings of my mind. So in the end I just said:

"To Marjorie, Pete and Katherine, who are all the people I love, this is my letter of resignation from *Neverending.com*. I'm sorry to do this. I wish my time here could also be never-ending. But unfortunately it can't. I bless the work you are doing. Joe."

At 3pm Stan gave me an envelope with the cash. For my part I sealed the letter of resignation, and gave it to him, along with the deed I had just signed.

"Take them over to the Plaza, will you Stan? Give them to Marjorie."

Stan nodded. I fancied I saw sadness in his eyes, which was nice, because Stan was not an overly emotional man.

Then I walked down to Grand Central and boarded a train to somewhere.

11.

The wealthiest Bra Boy in the world became a tramp, a hobo, a bum, a vagrant, a mendicant, a vagabond, a beggar. It's amazing how many names there are for you if you have no money.

I wandered about America for a while, spent half my money in the first month, and then got mugged in broad daylight outside a very refined coffee shop in Boulder Colorado. The mugger took the last of my cash. So I went into the cafe with blood pouring down my face from the gash on my forehead, sat down and bled into the sugar bowl.

The owner came over with a wad of gauze to stop the bleeding. She pressed it to my head, and apologized for what had happened to me right outside her shop. Then she called for a strong black coffee and a Danish.

"I've got no money to pay you," I said.

She told me not to worry. It was the least she could do to compensate for the bad name that mugger (who must have been from out of town) was giving to her genteel community.

It's interesting how scrumptious a coffee and a Danish can be when you realize they could be your last meal on earth. The thought comes to you pretty swiftly, when you have no cash, and no cards, and only the jeans and t-shirt you're wearing. Yes, this could be the last food I ever consume.

The owner sat down opposite me and asked how I had come to this predicament.

"I was Pete A Vanderveer's CEO at *Neverending.com*," I said, "but I fell in love with a woman I couldn't have. So I gave away all my money and shares, cut up all my credit cards, and hit the road with just a little cash in my pocket. The mugger took the last of that, so now I'm destitute."

She laughed a lot then (as did some other customers who overheard), and called for some more coffee. She said I must be suffering from concussion to think up a story like that.

After a while a middle aged man came over and asked to sit down. I said sure. I was happy to have some company. He was tallish and lean, with a close cropped beard and hair. He wore clothes that seemed to hang off him, and carried a small plastic bag with pictures of kittens on the outside.

"Is that really true?" he asked.

"About the mugging?"

"About Pete A Vanderveer and the money and the woman?"

"Yes, it is," I said.

"I thought so." He wore a sort of knowing smile. "Everyone assumed you were joking, but I could just tell. You don't make up stuff like that."

"I guess not," I said. I noticed that despite his rough appearance he spoke with quite a refined accent.

"What are you going to do?" he asked. I told him I had no idea. "You're pretty much a bum now," he ventured to tell me. "No offence of course."

"None taken," I assured him.

"I'm a bum," he told me, in a matter of fact tone.

"Really? You don't look like a bum."

"That's the trick," he explained. "I'm scruffy, but all sorts of people are scruffy, especially in a college town like this. The important thing is not to cross the line from looking scruffy to looking destitute."

"How do you manage that?" I was pretty keen to know. When all your money is gone you soon realize you might be needing some good advice. As a freshman bum, I was very pleased to hear the words of this senior.

"You make sure you have man's best friend," he smiled, pulling out a pair of tiny scissors, nail clippers I guessed. I nodded approvingly, though as yet having no idea where he was going with this. He continued: "The one thing that makes you look destitute is long greasy hair and beard. If you ask for something looking like that, you're sure to be knocked back, but if your hair and beard are trimmed close, you've got a chance. See for example, here I am in a classy cafe, sitting on one cup for half the day. But no-one tries to throw me out, because I'm the right side of the line.

"You're not going to be able to afford a razor and blades to stay clean shaven," he continued, "and you can't carry large scissors, because sooner or later the cops will take them off you. So you carry man's best friend and keep your hair and beard trimmed close with them."

"Must be time consuming," I ventured.

"It is, but then again you're going to have plenty of time."

"I guess so," I said.

"Unless of course you're just going to ring up Pete Vanderveer and get your old job back."

"No I really can't do that," I told him. "I'm going to be a bum for a while at least, I guess."

"Then take these," he said, passing the clippers over to me.

"I can't take man's best friend from you," I said. "What will you do for trimming?"

"I've got a second pair," he said. Then leaning closer and whispering: "Hidden in my shoe."

To this day I can't imagine how he walked, with any sort of comfort, if he had a pair of nail clippers in his boot. But that was neither here nor there. The important thing was this man had given up his most prized possession to a stranger. His sacrifice was enormous, not to mention his advice, which was beyond worth.

That was the day I learned you give what you can. And sometimes what you give, though it may appear insignificant to the world, can be magnificent.

That day too I learned the real value of a gift. It is measured, not in what you give, but in what you are giving up. Considering the risk he was taking, reducing himself to just one set of clippers, this man's gift was just as beautiful as a gift can be.

I thanked him profusely. We both stood and formally shook hands. He wished me all the best in my new career as a bum, and hoped we would run into each other again soon, if I chose to stay on in Boulder. I thought I probably would. It was summer, and the mountain weather was beautiful. It seemed like as good a place as any to begin my apprenticeship.

"What's your name?" I called after him as he was walking away.

"Arthur T. Arthurson," he called back.

"Interesting name," I smiled.

"What's yours?"

"Joe Stalin," I heard myself say.

"You should talk," he laughed.

I sat for a while in the coffee shop, watching

the other customers. There is a heightened awareness that comes with being on the edge of survival. All the distractions, great and small, melt away. Their place is taken by the essentials of food and shelter. You look at your fellows in the coffee shop and realize they aren't thinking about those things. But you are. You most certainly are.

My first thought was where will I sleep tonight? Of course I had no idea. I didn't even know where to start. I had lived a life where each step I took was planned. But how can you plan when the permutations of your life are completely unknown? So I did what I guessed all bums would do. I left the coffee shop and started to wander, looking for some sort of inspiration.

After about an hour's walking I noticed Sts Peter and Paul Catholic Church. It was a modern style building with a large arched portico area at the front. I remembered that I had once been a Catholic. I didn't really want to trade on that. It would feel very hypocritical, as I'd had nothing to do with the Church since I threw my Vegemite sandwiches at Father Meany in Year 11 and stormed out of the school never to return.

At the same time I realized pride would have to be the first victim of my life as a bum. I would have to take any chance I could find, or manufacture. As I walked up to the church I wondered if there were a pattern developing in my life. Father Meany had copped the Vegemite sandwiches because he'd caught me kissing Meg

Nelson behind the science block after class. He had tried to forbid me from seeing her again. So I'd vegemited him and taken off. Was my life destined to be a series of thwarted loves followed by extreme flight? I put the thought from my mind as I stepped up to the presbytery.

The priest who came to the door was a very young man. He had a thick accent, Filipino I guessed.

"Good evening, Father," I said. "My name is Joe Stalin and I'm a bum."

"You don't look like a bum," he said.

"Well I'm just starting out."

He looked at me as though he was unsure whether this was a joke, but in the end just said:

"What can I do for you?"

"I don't have anywhere to sleep tonight, and I was wondering if you have a spare stable." He stared at me then, so I added: "I am a Catholic, but I have to be honest. I haven't been to mass since I threw my Vegemite sandwiches at Father Meany."

I don't know why I said that. Maybe it was nerves. I'd never begged before. But I felt like I was suffering from some sort of Tourette Syndrome, because I wanted to blurt out more. In fact I felt I couldn't stop myself.

"It was all because of Meg Nelson," I was continuing, when he held up his hand to stop me.

"You don't have to be a Catholic. You are welcome," and now he bathed me in the whitest smile I had ever seen. "We don't have a stable, but there may be a spot on the portico."

It turned out that every night, once the evening mass was over, Father Njhay would make the portico available to the town bums to sleep on. He explained there was a strict seniority list, and I would have to apply for a spot to the most senior bum. He gave me a sleeping bag then and took me round to wait on the portico for the other bums to arrive.

"This is your sleeping bag now," he said. "For you to keep."

"That is very generous. Are you sure?"

"Oh yes," he insisted, "we have a family group which raises money for sleeping bags."

"Is that right?" There was so much going on in the world beyond the Avenue of the Americas.

"They are very active," he said with pride.

"Who is the senior bum?" I asked.

"We prefer to call them homeless people," he gently corrected me.

"Yes of course. Sorry. Who is the senior homeless person?"

"His name is Arthur," The priest told me.

"Not Arthur T. Arthurson?"

He thought for a moment and then said: "I am embarrassed to admit I don't know his second name."

But then to my infinite delight the Arthur in question was my Arthur. For he soon arrived leading a group of about a dozen other homeless men and women, as though they were his disciples, coming back from the sea of Galilea. He strode out ahead of them, expostulating loudly and waving his arms about.

I had never been so happy to see anyone. For his part he seemed pleased to see me.

"Joe Stalin," he exclaimed, taking my hand and shaking it firmly. Then to the disciples. "This is my friend Joe Stalin. But not *the* Joe Stalin. At least I don't think so."

"*The* Joe Stalin was my father," I said.

Two or three of the disciples took a fearful step backward, and so I explained I was only kidding. I resolved to keep my Tourette Syndrome under control.

I explained to Arthur that Father Njhay had given me a sleeping bag and told me to apply to him for a spot. He looked quite distressed.

"There isn't actually a spot at the moment, Joe," he apologized. He thought for a moment, then said: "But it's summer and it doesn't rain so much in Boulder. Why not sleep on the steps? I'm sure Father Njhay won't mind." Then he brightened and added: "Someone is bound to have died before winter, and you'll be first on the list."

As the evening darkened Father Njhay came out with some plates of food for everyone. I was amazed.

"It's easier being a bum than I thought," I said to Arthur.

"Depends where you are," he replied. "Here

in Boulder it's pretty good. But I knew someone who froze to death on a bench right outside the main entrance to Union Station in Denver. He just went to sleep and didn't wake up. Mind you it was so cold he didn't start to smell for days, so he just lay there while people filed by morning and night."

If I had started to get complacent, that rocked me back into place.

"It also depends on the people," he added. "If Father Njhay gets transferred and another priest comes in, we could all be out of here tomorrow. You are at the mercy of the fates," he said, philosophically.

"I guess that's true of everyone," I ventured.

"Yes, Joe, You're right. But people with money have the illusion of being in control."

"I couldn't control how Katherine felt," I found myself saying out of nowhere.

I realized it was the first time I had really thought about her. By some miracle I had kept the person who most mattered to me out of my conscious mind for a whole month. Then at Arthur's mention of 'control' she popped back. Who knows why? But now, I was pretty sure, she wasn't going to leave any time soon.

"Was that her name? Nice name Katherine. Honest name."

"She *was* honest," I said. It seemed strange to refer to her in the past tense. But the present tense would have been stranger.

We talked for a little longer, but then as night fell, everyone took their assigned places on the portico, whilst I settled down on the steps. My first night as a bum was a big starry night. I fell asleep looking at the stars and thinking of Katherine.

12.

I spent almost a year in Boulder Colorado. In that time I became second in charge to Arthur T. Arthurson, just as I had been to Marcellus Vanderveer and then to his son. It seemed to be my lot in life. But I really didn't mind. I saw it as a privilege to 'work' for remarkable people.

I discovered Arthur had been an actor in his day. He had worked on the main stage theaters in Chicago and Off-Broadway in New York City. He had even had some small parts in a few films. But one day, tired of the struggle that is the lot of most actors, he fired his agent, tore up his headshots and hit the road. In its heightened and unmistakable sense of drama, it was a lot like how I had abandoned my life's work. It gave us a sense of camaraderie.

The reason I quickly became his second in charge in the world of Boulder hobos, was that Arthur and I were really the only two who didn't suffer from a mental illness. Now this is a delicate subject. What is mental illness after all? Many would say Arthur and I, in throwing away our former lives, had significant problems.

But I am talking about mental illness as the medical profession sees it. Arthur and I would not have been diagnosable, however eccentric the world may have seen us. But the other portico dwellers at Sts Peter and Paul were pretty much all certifiable. That is because most people only become portico dwellers if they *do* have a mental illness. Very few people actually choose to be homeless.

Some of the disciples suffered depression, some were bi-polar, but the majority suffered from schizophrenia which, as I was to learn, carries a terrible stigma in society, even though it is a physiological brain disorder, as treatable as a cut on the hand.

Unfortunately for the schizophrenics, they didn't see themselves as having a disorder and in need of treatment. The voices they heard in their heads were as real to them as the voice of Father Njhay, only rarely as benign.

Sometimes I would lay awake at night on the steps and listen to someone having a heated conversation with one of their voices. Mostly it was incomprehensible, but one woman, Maggie, produced a running narrative that was as good as a radio serial.

I was told Maggie was around 45 years old, but she looked 20 years older. She had been singled out by a dominant race of semi-metallic creatures called Tangoids. The Tangoids had come down to earth, not surprisingly, to take it over, and make it a better place. Unfortunately the 'take-over' was going to be bloody. It was Maggie's job to follow the orders of the Tangoids and assist them in their quest.

Naturally enough the Tangoids had forbidden Maggie from telling anyone about this, especially the authorities. If she did, horrible things would happen to her. So naturally she was never going to get medication because she was never going to see a doctor.

I knew all this, not just from overhearing her midnight conversations with the Tangoids, but because for some inexplicable reason they allowed her to confide in me. I can't begin to guess why I was so privileged, but the upshot was every other night she would be down on the step filling me in on her latest instructions.

"Tomorrow I have to go into town," she would say, "to the butchers. There is a side of lamb there that is dangerous. I have to uplift it. I have to spirit it away."

"Don't do it, Maggie," I tried to gently warn. "The butcher will get angry."

"I know, I know," she said, sadly shaking her head. "But what choice do I have. If I forsake my duty, all could be lost."

I quickly learned to listen and not try to prevent. My arguments were never going to prevail over the Tangoids. It was all quite hopeless really. Maggie would go and attempt to 'uplift' the lamb. Of course the butcher would catch her. The police would be called. She would spend a night in gaol, but when the doctor or psych would be called she would go quiet and just say she had tried to steal the lamb because she was hungry. The judge would give her a very short sentence or a suspended sentence and then she would return again to the portico at Sts Peter and Paul, and all the disciples would welcome her back.

Sometimes, at night, the voices of more than one disciple would start to run at the same time. You could then hear what sounded like a conversation between two people but where there was no connection between what the two 'interlocutors' had to say, unless of course your imagination could supply some meaning:

"But what if the butcher catches me?"

"Of course there is no need to tell me that."

"But he might hit me."

"Ha! Ha! Harrumph then!"

"Of course I will do what you tell me."

"Good, good, good, good, good, then now!"

Sometimes I felt like I was listening to a sort of Chaucerian romp. But to the conversationalists it was a great deal more serious than that. One thing seemed a constant: the voices which possessed these people had no sense of humor. They had their obsessive needs, which their 'vessels/vassals' had to play out, and there would be no time for rest.

I couldn't imagine what it must have been like for Maggie and the others, trying to cope with those voices in their heads, the incessant, obsessive driving voices. I understood a little better when Arthur arranged a practical demonstration for me. He got two of the disciples with rolled up newspapers which they put to each of my ears. Arthur told me to think of something I would like to try to explain to the others, something simple within my own knowledge.

I settled on explaining some basic concepts around book marketing. As I began to speak the two disciples with the rolled up newspapers started to speak down them into my ears, saying things like:

"What a load of nonsense! What are you trying to say? That's wrong. That's wrong. You don't want to say that. Dumbhead! Dumbhead!"

And the more I tried to block out their words the more insistent they became. At no point was I able to get out even a part of my planned explanation, not even a sentence without stumbling on my words and getting more and more angry and confused. In the end all I wanted to do was cry. I had no desire to tell my story any more. I just wanted to give the voices whatever they wanted, so they would leave me alone.

But as Arthur explained, they were never going to leave me alone, not until they had secured their perfect and exquisite destruction of me.

The disciples had their times of 'sanity' however, or at least that's how it seemed from the outside. For example when the voices left her alone, Maggie was a warm, sensitive and sensible woman. She had had a good education and a strong family life. But the Tangoids had taken all that from her. Now her only protection was going to be from Father Njhay, Arthur, and perhaps myself. But we could do little, for our influence could never match that of the Tangoids.

When Maggie was free of her voices I would try to talk her into getting some help. She would say she would think about it, but my sense was that even in her 'lucid' moments the Tangoids were still lurking somewhere in the background, and she feared defying them. In the end she would never seek the help she needed, and her life continued to spiral down, as she got more and more skinny and unhealthy, for the Tangoids left little time for nourishment, of the body or of the mind.

One night Maggie didn't come back. We waited, but several nights passed and we all knew we had seen the last of her. Arthur said she would have died. That may or may not have been true. But we all wanted to think so. As harsh as that sounds, we saw it as the preferable option. No-one wanted to imagine her wandering the world without even the protection of Arthur and Father Njhay. For then who knows what might happen to her.

It was October when she disappeared and Arthur invited me up onto the portico to take her spot.

"I said someone was sure to die before winter," he reminded me.

I thought for a long while about it. I didn't want to take Maggie's spot. It was her spot not mine. And if I did, it was like closing the option of her ever coming back. But then we lived a life where survival touched finger tips with destruction, and where sentiment could be the falsest of friends.

So I moved up onto the portico, and Arthur made a little speech to the disciples, officially welcoming me to the community of Sts Peter and Paul, even though I had lived amongst them for nearly three months. Everyone applauded and then went to sleep.

Once there, without Arthur ever making a formal declaration, everyone accepted I was second in charge. It was as though, on some level, they knew I was the only one, apart from Arthur, who was sane enough for the job.

It wasn't all that tricky. It just meant when Arthur wasn't there, it was up to me to make decisions. It could be as simple as moving everyone back further under the shelter of the portico as the weather got colder. Or maybe we needed to swap positions so someone sick could get the warmth of one person on either side of her. Simple, logical, survival based decisions – not unlike the best way to run a business. Not unlike the way Pete and I ran *Neverending.com.*

In fact I soon realized life was life, wherever and however you lived it. The life of the corporate billionaire is more complex, but then the corporate billionaire has thousands of people to help him. In either case it comes down to survival, or not. The hobo freezes to death on a bench outside Union Station, the billionaire drops dead walking the hill on the 8th fairway.

For Arthur and myself survival depended on how we used our minds and our talents. I guess that applied to all of us, but Arthur and I could go about the task of our survival a little more systematically than most.

Right from the beginning I had realized Father Njhay's modest evening meal was going to need supplementing. I had also quickly learnt pride was a luxury. So I accepted Arthur's advice and approached the cafe owner where I had been mugged to see if she could manage a regular Danish and a coffee each morning. I was amazed at how easily she agreed. Arthur said it was because people find it hard to say no when they've shared something with you, particularly something as dramatic as a mugging.

Of course some mornings there were a lot of customers and all the pastries sold out, and then I would have to go without. When that happened I made it my business to accept the situation with grace and to thank her anyway.

My back up was that Arthur too had his friendly cafe, where he would wait in the back lane each morning, and the big hearted chef would bring him something without the owner's knowledge. If my Danish were not forthcoming, Arthur would share his stash with me. And when he lucked out I would share my Danish with him.

It's hard to describe the strength of the bond that sort of arrangement engenders. It is beyond friendship as the modern world understands it. Maybe it's something like it was in primitive times, when the whole village depended on the hunter or the gatherer. Arthur and I were hunters (or was it gatherers?) who totally depended on one another.

And that sort of dependence means you do truly love your neighbor as yourself, because your survival depends on that neighbor. Arthur and I were neighbors in every sense. We slept with our bodies side by side and we worked together to keep our respective bodies alive.

Early on too, I had also decided to try my luck with the bookshop owner whose shop was right next to the cafe. It was a big bright bookshop stocked with a world of titles. It looked great to the customers, but I knew he was overstocked for the sort of market he had, even in a college town.

I wandered about the shelves and could identify hundreds of books that would be slow selling titles. They were probably on sale or return, but the cash flow problem would be crushing. Then if they didn't sell at all, he would have the cost of returning them.

I asked Arthur if I should offer my services, and he said of course I should. Any angle was worth exploiting. So I went to the bathroom at Sts Peter and Paul, made sure man's best friend did its job, and called on the bookseller.

He was a tall, extremely gaunt man, with exaggerated horn rim glasses. He looked like he was about to audition for a Dickensian character in the local community theater production. I later learned he *was* an amateur thespian, who no doubt thought the image he had created for himself was appropriate for a bookseller in a college town.

"Hi," I said, extending my hand, which he took with some trepidation. "My name's Joe Stalin and I used to work for Marcellus Vanderveer and then his son Pete as their CEO. So I know quite a bit about books. Now I would be willing to advise you how to get your cash flow crisis back in order, if you could just pay me a small stipend. What about we look at a weekly meeting, for say $50 per hour?"

I gave him my biggest smile. It didn't however provoke a smile in return. He just looked at me for a long time, or should I say looked down at me over the top of his glasses. He was obviously trying to assess if there were even the vaguest chance of my patter being true.

Of course he had heard of the bookselling legend, even as far west as Boulder.

"You didn't work for Marcellus," he said in the end, and quite dismissively too.

I then reeled off a series of facts and details about Marcellus and his sales techniques only someone who knew him and knew the business could possibly know.

After a long hesitation, Henry, for that was the bookseller's name, said:

"I can't afford to give you cash, but I can pay you in books."

Arthur had been hanging about the shelves listening. He now chose this moment to buy into the negotiations:

"Could you make sure he got plays and books of poetry?"

"Sure," Henry said. "And you are?"

"I'm his agent," Arthur laughed, and Henry almost laughed too, but not quite.

In any event the deal was done. Each Tuesday morning I would come in and advise Henry on what to purchase and what not, on quantities and acceptable discounts. In a short space of time his business was staring to turn around and Arthur and I had a collection of poems and plays three feet high sitting in the corner of the portico at Sts Peter and Paul.

Such was my respect for Arthur, I never thought to ask why he wanted payment in poems and plays. I just assumed he would have a very good reason. In fact he had more than a reason – he had a plan!

"We're going to be buskers," he told me one morning, "strolling players, if you will."

Arthur's idea was that we would pick some poetry and some scenes from plays, learn them off and act them out in the Pearl Street Mall. He said as the weather was getting colder, it would be a great way to keep warm. We were going to be a 'physical theater' troupe.

I was a little reluctant. I had never acted before, and doubted if I could. But Arthur told me I had natural stage presence, which was good to know. What's more he would train me in all the finer points of the Stanislavski Method.

"I studied under Lee Strasberg," he told me, "right near the end of his life." Then he confessed: "But only for a couple of weeks till he realized I didn't have the money to pay him. So he threw me out. But not before I had absorbed The Method. Well, a little bit of The Method." He thought for a moment, smiled and said: "Mainly I trained myself. But don't we all, Joe?"

"I think we do," I had to admit.

We had been standing on the portico and I watched Arthur take off his coat and throw it on the ground.

"The body of Caesar," he proclaimed, pointing to the coat. And when I must have looked confused: "No better time to start than the present. Are you familiar with Marc Antony's oration over the body of Caesar?"

"Friends, Romans, Countrymen?" I ventured.

"That comes later. Right now Caesar has just been hacked to death by the ambitious and duplicitous Brutus and Cassius. Caesar was the most powerful man in Rome. He was also my 'father', my mentor, and my greatest friend. As his 'son' I, Antony, was the second most powerful man in Rome. My future was assured. But now I have just seen him butchered. I can do nothing to avenge him, at least not now. Brutus and Cassius have all the cards. In fact if I even so much as question their actions, I will be hacked to death myself.

"So I stand there like an impotent buffoon, waiting for them to leave. Then when alone with Caesar, all I can do is apologize and swear to avenge him when he time is right."

I watched as Arthur circled the coat, eventually squatting down next to it, talking to it in the softest, most hopeless and apologetic voice I had ever heard, tears already running down his cheeks.

"*O pardon me, thou bleeding piece of earth,*
That I am meek and gentle with these butchers."

He quietly spat out the word 'butchers' in a way that made me shudder, physically shudder.

"*Thou art the ruins of the noblest man*
That ever lived in the tide of times.
I curse to the hands that shed this costly blood."

Now he was up and walking, thinking, planning, cursing, finally coming back to stand over the lifeless body of his beloved father. It had long since ceased to be a coat, and had become, for me, the audience, the blood-stained body of Caesar.

"Over thy wounds, now do I prophesy."

And his voice began to build, towards an inevitable crescendo.

"A curse shall light upon the limbs of men.
Blood and destruction shall be so in use,
And dreadful objects so familiar,
That mothers shall but smile when they behold
Their infants quartered by the hands of war."

Arthur smiled then at the thought of this impossibly gruesome scenario, and the intensity of my shudder doubled.

"All pity choked with custom of fell deed."

Now Arthur was silent for a long time, assessing Caesar, assessing the future. And in that silence the crescendo of his voice was never lost. It returned as the voice of vengeance, bred from absolute despair.

"And Caesar's spirit, ranging for revenge,
With Ate by his side come hot from hell,
Shall, in these confines, with a monarch's voice,"

Now he was down on his knees besides his dead hero, begging for his forgiveness, praying to the Gods above, with his warrior's arms thrust upward:

"Cry HAVOC!"

I had never heard a human voice project with such volume and such power. The very portico shook beneath and around us. But now his voice shrank to a bitter, merciless determination:

"And let slip the dogs of war.
That this foul deed shall smell above the earth
With carrion men, groaning for burial."

Arthur collapsed beside his dead hero, as though he were dead himself. The tears were rolling down my own cheeks. After a little while I remembered that I had not been watching Marc Antony and the body of Caesar, but rather my friend and fellow hobo, Arthur T. Arthurson, talking to his coat.

"How did you do that?" I asked in astonishment.

Arthur sat up and smiled:

"It's called acting," he said.

"You are a great actor," I said.

"I'm ok," he humbly confessed. "But there are hundreds who could do it just as well. And most of them are better looking than me." He smiled again. "That's why I chose a life beneath the stars. But here in Boulder, I might be good enough to get us a few pennies in the Mall, with your help of course."

"I could never do that," I insisted.

"You will, soon," he assured me. "But in the meantime you can just play the body of Caesar."

"That won't keep me very warm," I laughed. "But you still haven't answered me. How do you do it? How do you act like that?"

Arthur looked about, as though making sure no-one would overhear him.

"The secret to acting," he said, "is NOT to act, but to believe. If I believe then I am not deceiving my audience, I am telling them the truth. I am being honest. It's all about honesty. I didn't act being Marc Antony. I *was* Marc Antony. I truly believed I *was* the general."

"I believed it too," I said.

"If I believe, you will believe. If I pretend, you will feel nothing."

"How do I believe?" I asked, feeling like a novice beseeching his preacher for the key to faith.

"Emotion memory," he told me. "I can't guess what Marc Antony felt 2000 years ago. But I remember what it was like when my grandfather died. He was my greatest friend, my biggest supporter, and he was taken from me far too early, just when I needed him the most. When I play Marc Antony I remember my grandfather. The emotion you see is the real grief for my grandfather, remembered all over again."

"That must be exhausting," I suggested.

"It is. And it's dangerous. For some actors when the show is over the emotion remains. Theirs is a life on which the curtain never falls, where the emotions of their life blend seamlessly with the emotions of all their characters, till they live a life that belongs exclusively to their muse and not to themselves."

"Did that ever happen to you."

"Another reason why I left the trade," he smiled.

"Might you get locked into Marc Antony right there in the Pearl St Mall?"

"I hope not," he said. "But if you see it happening, just improvise Julius Caesar back to life and slap me one."

Then my tutelage as an actor began. Arthur taught me how to create a backstory for my character to help bring it to life, taught me how to project my voice, taught me the tricks for learning lines quickly and easily, and most importantly of all, taught me how to claim the stage.

We developed a huge, eclectic and varied repertoire, which we progressively put into action in the Pearl Street Mall. We did some more Shakespeare, some Ibsen and some Chekhov. We even did Blanche and Stanley from *A Streetcar Named Desire*. As the junior member of the troupe, I played Blanche.

We also performed poetry, sometimes as solos, sometimes as a duet. Many of the great poets of the English language found themselves revitalized in the cool of the Pearl Street Mall in Boulder Colorado that autumn.

For my part I taught Arthur about Banjo Patterson and his idyll to his stockman *Clancy of the Overflow*, which ends with Patterson's immortal words:

"And I somehow rather fancy that I'd like to change with Clancy, like to take a turn at droving where the seasons come and go, while he faced the round eternal of the cash-book and the journal.

But I doubt he'd suit the office, Clancy of `The Overflow'."

Arthur was really taken with this Aussie bush yarn.

"Are we like Clancy?" he asked me. "Do we scorn the Pattersons of the world, trapped in their mean little clerical jobs?"

"Well first of all Patterson was a wealthy lawyer, and Clancy's life, had Clancy existed, would have been short and hard, and full of heat, dust and flies."

"Ah, well," said Arthur, "such is the power of fiction."

But Clancy became part of our repertoire too, and he, like so many others came to life again, far from their homes in Russia, Norway, England, Australia, and the early frontier of the United States.

We started out doing weekends only. For hours we would toil away and a few passers-by would throw a few pennies into Arthur's cap. I say toil, but it was anything but hard work for me. I loved it. Arthur had given me the gift of whole other worlds, where Joe Stalin could escape the shackles of Joe Stalin and become Eilert Løvborg, Macbeth, Clancy of the Overflow, and of course Blanche DuBois.

For weeks, though we poured every drop of our passion into our characters, the residents of Boulder and the tourists would saunter by, paying us little attention. Then one Saturday morning, amidst the bustling shoppers, Arthur's Stanley screamed "Stella!" and people stopped and began to listen. A small circle formed around us, which grew bigger and bigger as we jumped from *Hedda Gabler* to *The Cherry Orchard* and joyously backed to *Streetcar* again.

As the sun was setting we counted our takings. A Saturday would normally yield about $10. This time we had over $200. I couldn't understand what had changed.

"It's not something anyone can explain," Arthur told me. "But if you keep your product out there long enough, sometimes the collective unconscious of your audience expands just enough to tip over into success. Enough people walked by us often enough, and absorbed what we were doing just enough times, that when I threw down the taper of 'Stella!', the fire of interest in the Joe and Arthur theater company was alight."

"I'm not sure I get it," I told him, "but it sure sounds poetic the way you tell it."

"It's the problem with so many plays," he continued. "Their run ends before the taper is alight."

"Same with books," I said. "By the time enough interest has gathered, the booksellers have sent the copies back. Unless of course you are an author lucky enough to have Marcellus Vanderveer in your corner."

"Pete's father?"

"Yes," I told him. "A great bookseller, and a great friend."

I started to tear-up, and felt very silly. But Arthur didn't press me. Instead he said:

"Our run is not limited. We have the stage of life, right here in the Pearl Street Mall, as long as we like."

"That is good," I agreed.

Our success that Saturday afternoon proved not to be fleeting. Now the word had spread and we were making $200 every Saturday, and Sundays too. What's more we developed a student audience and so played 'matinees' for them through the week.

After a while Henry the bookseller asked if he could act with us. He wasn't very good. Arthur explained he was an 'outside in' actor, which was the exact opposite of The Method, which was 'inside out'. He said amateurs were usually outside in, but they were also stubborn and there was no way of changing them. So we kept him to smallish parts, like the body of Caesar. But he seemed happy enough, and all his customers and friends from the community theater came along, which swelled the takings.

We looked like we were in for a long run at the Boulder Open Air Theatorium, as we called it. But life has a way of getting in the way. I had only just finished joking with Arthur:

"I'd hardly call us strolling players, unless you count every morning's stroll from the church to the Mall."

Then we were face to face with the face of authority. We were half way through Eilert Løvborg's moment of truth with Hedda Gabler (I was playing Hedda), when a gentleman from the Boulder City Council strode onto the stage, unfortunately determined to play himself. He told us we were unlicensed buskers and the show was over.

The audience, I am delighted to say, booed him incessantly, some even labelling him a fascist dictator. But he was unmoved, and so we were the ones who had to move.

We went back to the portico only to find that our beloved Father Njhay was gone. The Bishop had discovered all about *his* unlicensed activities, to wit his unauthorized use of church property to shelter the disciples.

Poor Father Njhay was whisked away without even the chance to say goodbye. His replacement had much in common with the City Council's fascist dictator, only in robes. He made a long self-justifying speech to Arthur and I and the gathered disciples that night, terminating with the termination of our portico lease. We were told we had one more night, but after that, whilst we were always welcome to worship with him, we were not to sleep on his porch.

Arthur and I had lost our livelihood and our accommodation all in one day, and the winter was coming on. But at least we now had bankable skills. The real problem was the disciples. They were distraught. We were distraught for them. They had come to rely on Father Njhay. Now suddenly he was gone. Some of them were in tears as we settled down for the night. For several others, that night, their conversations with their imaginary friends took on far greater intensity.

In the morning Arthur gathered them together on the lawn of the church. We had already been ejected from the portico. He explained there was not much he or I could do for them. Their time as a clan was over. A group so large would always be rejected by anyone they approached. Their only option was to look for help in ones and twos.

He suggested several charities, cafes and shops around town they might approach. I felt sick in my stomach. Of course I had no confidence in their abilities to look after themselves. Nonetheless each in their own way had found Father Njhay. Perhaps they could find their way to someone else who would give them a place to be at peace, or as much peace as their problems would allow.

Arthur and I had made almost $6000 from our busking. He took it all out and divided it equally amongst the disciples, keeping just $100 for us. Then he told them we were leaving and we walked away to the sounds of sniffling and muffled crying. I thought my heart would break, but I knew Arthur was right. We had nothing to offer them apart from the money. Our job was to work out a way to earn it all over again.

"*Now* we are strolling players," Arthur suggested, as we walked out towards the edge of town, with little beyond our sleeping bags and our $100. "But you know, Joe, we are very lucky," he said. "We have our theater company and we are not crazy. What's more we are free."

"A little freer than I would have liked," I ventured.

"Can you have too much freedom?" he asked, smiling at me with all the charm of Eilert Løvborg.

"I guess not, Arthur," I said.

13.

"I was hoping if we did have to stroll, we could stroll by train," Arthur reflected, as we stood together by the roadside, trying to thumb a lift.

"Is this going to work?" I asked. "When I was a teenager in Australia I hitchhiked a lot. But that was before a lot of honest drivers got murdered. Then no-one would pick us up."

"Much the same here," Arthur said, " but there are still some people who'll give a hitchhiker a ride."

"What about two middle aged hitchhikers who look the worse for wear?"

"You're not middle aged." he said.

"I feel middle aged, and I'm sure the average motorist…"

"We'll just have to wait," Arthur said, to put an end to such fruitless conversation.

We did wait, for around eight hours, but in the end an old drunk in a pickup truck stopped for us just after midnight, and drove us all the way to Santa Fe. It was a miracle we got there alive, for during the whole six hour trip he didn't seem to sober up, even a little. But alive we were at seven in the morning on a cool December day. Our driver dropped us right in Santa Fe's beautiful Old Town Square, which we knew at once would make a perfect open air theater.

As we strolling players strolled about the square and the town, I watched Arthur's directorial eye focus on every detail.

"Promenade theater!" he exclaimed with delight. "We'll do promenade theater. Look at all the levels, and the spaces, and the runs."

I, of course, had no idea what he was talking about. But I enjoyed watching Arthur's enthusiasm, and I knew he would explain later, which he did. This beautiful, light, 400 year old square, with its feeder streets just made to lead the audience right to us, was going to be the biggest stage we had ever played.

We would use the whole square, the monument, the bandstand, the seats and benches, to change our levels, to keep the audience guessing. We would be running across the street to the ancient colonnades and dancing midst the sellers of trinkets and wares. We would hide behind the winter trees just enough to be seen, and we would carry the spirit of Santa Fe's founding Franciscan Padres into the four corners of our theatrical world.

What's more the audience would move along with us. Promenade theater! Wherever we went they would be there too, moving, always moving with us.

"It's what real theater should be," Arthur told me. "Everyone involved. Shakespeare would approve. No soft seats and heating to send them to sleep. It just can't fail."

And it didn't. Unlike Boulder, where we had to build an audience slowly, here we had them hooked immediately. We started around midday on the day we arrived, because we had no time to lose. We had almost no money, and nowhere to stay.

We began with a sword fight scene from Othello. Of course we had no swords, and we certainly didn't substitute. As Arthur explained: "If we believe we have swords, though our hands be empty, the audience will believe it too. But if we whack each other with sticks, the audience will just see us whacking each other with sticks."

The audience loved it. They cheered and followed us as we cursed in Elizabethan English and drove one another back and forth across the Old Town Square. As I fell dying beneath the thrust of Arthur's invisible sword, a roar went up from the crowd and I felt more alive than I ever had.

When the show was over and the audience started to disperse, a dark haired woman who looked in her late forties, strode purposefully up to us.

"Good afternoon, gents," she said, in a crisp tone. "I'm Di Delorenzo. I'm a lawyer and the mayor of the City of Santa Fe."

Our hearts sank. Already we were going to be thrown out, and this time not even by a city official, but by the mayor herself.

"You boys just arrived in town?"

"That's right," Arthur said. Already we were metaphorically hoisting our sleeping bags onto our shoulders.

"Well aren't we lucky?" she said, a huge smile covering her face. "Got somewhere to stay?"

"Not yet," I confessed, not quite believing where this seemed to be going.

"How would you like to live in the oldest house in the U.S.A.?" she said. "It's an old adobe house just down on East De Vargas Street. Belongs to the city. We're going to make it into a museum, but right now it's empty. No heating, no running water, no facilities at all. What do you say?"

"Sounds perfect," Arthur said. "Is it really the oldest house in the country?"

"Of course other towns make similar claims." She spoke dismissively of these frauds. "But we know ours is the oldest."

"We would be honored," I said.

"Now what about these performances?" The mayor got straight to the point. "Can we expect a daily show, varied format? Are we in a position to advertise to the tourists?" I think we must have both just stared at her, because she quickly added: "Can't pay you much of course. Not more than $100 per show, but then you get to keep what the public throws in your hat. What do you say?" There was that huge smile again.

"We say yes!" Arthur told her.

"Good, good," she beamed. "Now how about some classic American repertoire? Or a little historical drama set in the south west, maybe New Mexico, maybe on the Santa Fe Trail? Not that I want to interfere with your artistic integrity."

"Mayor, if you are paying us, and you want it, we'll do Moby Dick with Joe playing the great white whale, beached in the New Mexico desert."

"That would be interesting," she laughed. "Let's keep it on the back burner."

So there we were, no more than half a day after arriving in Santa Fe by death defying pickup truck. We had accommodation, we had paid employment, and we had the respect and support of the town mayor. As we sat on the earthen floor of our new home that night, I said to Arthur:

"I don't think we can claim to be bums anymore?"

"That is true," he agreed, "we can afford

razors now. That is the line one crosses back into respectability."

"I'm still keeping man's best friend."

"Very wise my fellow troubadour," Arthur exclaimed. "Life can be capricious. One would be foolish to forget man's best friend."

We slept long and deeply that night. In the morning we began our new career as Santa Fe's semi-official promenade street theater troupe. Most days the mayor would drop by and see what we were performing. She always seemed pleased, but equally she always had a suggestion to make. However on the basis of Arthur's great white whale in the desert metaphor, we were more than happy to play it any way she chose.

Before we knew it we had been in Santa Fe all through the winter and spring, and now were performing to large crowds of summer tourists in and around the Old Town Square. We had mattresses and an oil burner in our adobe home. We had new clothes. We were clean shaven and we bought all our own food.

Most amazingly (and here we struggled with our moral position), we had a bank account. It did seem to run counter to the hobo's code, but we were starting to make real money, and my experience of being mugged in broad daylight in Boulder, convinced us to make this one concession.

Most mornings, before we went down to perform, we would take a coffee and something small to eat at the Cafe of the Holy Ghost, right near our house. We loved it. The owner, Pedro, treated us like celebrities. He baked his own biscuits and cookies, and was always giving us a new one to try.

There was a small television set up on the wall which always ran quietly in the background. One morning as we sat trying Pedro's latest hot baked cookie, I found myself calling out to him:

"Quick, Pedro, turn it up will you?"

It was Pete and Katherine. They were being interviewed on a morning show. I couldn't believe it. They were so real up there on the screen, so recognizable to me, and yet so far away from the life I had led over the last two years.

"Yes we *are* in the business of ending world poverty and disease," Pete was saying. "That is our real business. The other businesses are no longer businesses for their own sake. They are a means to an end."

He spoke with a confidence and a serenity which had grown even stronger since last I saw him.

"What do the shareholders think about that?" the interviewer asked him.

"They're in the business of ending world poverty and disease too."

"Quite a sacrifice for them. How did you get them on board?"

"No sacrifice. The other businesses are doing better than ever. People want to trade with us.

People trust us because of what we are doing in the Third World."

The interviewer was caught between admiration and skepticism.

"Sounds too good to be true," she ventured.

"It is true," Pete said, with a simplicity and a sincerity which must have been as irresistible to every member of that television audience as it was to me.

I looked across at Arthur.

"That's her? That's your Katherine?"

"Not *my* Katherine," I said. And now it was Katherine who was speaking, in her beautiful lilting, almost lost Australian accent.

"Yes we are spending billions," she was answering. "But it is an investment in the future prosperity of the world, and as *Neverending.com* is part of the world, it is an investment in us too."

"Smart as well as beautiful," Arthur was whispering.

"That's the only sort I ever fall in love with," I smiled back at him.

"And now you're on a mission, to enlist other billionaires?" the interviewer was asking Katherine.

"We are," Katherine said. "We can't do it alone."

"But even if you got every rich person in the world on board, surely the task is too great, too expensive?"

"It's not, you know," Pete answered her. "In

fact if you do the sums you'll see. Divide the cost of curing poverty and disease by the revenue of the world's largest companies, and those companies are still left with a healthy profit. Healthy enough to keep all their shareholders as comfortable as they could ever require. What's more, by saving all those lives and eliminating all that poverty, they've just got themselves a whole new loyal market."

It was almost word for word what Katherine had said that day at the Mount Lavinia Beach Hotel in Sri Lanka. They really were a team, I thought.

"That simple?" the interviewer asked, smiling at them both.

"That simple," they responded in unison.

And then they were gone. I was conscious of Arthur looking at me, but I didn't want to look at him. I didn't trust my response. I didn't know what my response would be. I got up and went to the bathroom.

I stood there looking at myself in the mirror, and was surprised at what I saw. It was someone who still loved Katherine, but who was glad about what she and Pete were doing. What a long way they had come since that day in Colombo when Pete had scowled about the corridors of the Home for the Dying.

In just a few short years, their mission had grown to something the world had never quite seen. That world had known many great philanthropists, but their work had always been a sideline. No-one had ever made it the central focus of their work. No-one had ever taken on the task of enlisting others to the cause. That was unique. That had the potential to change the world.

The face in the mirror even allowed itself just a little pride. After all I had started it off. Admittedly I had given one million dollars to a charity I didn't even understand to impress a woman I had fallen in love with way too quickly. But it was that act which had begun what the world was now starting to see. I remembered something Father Njhay had said:

"The Lord uses everyone, and it matters not what they intend. It matters only what He achieves with them."

As a lapsed Catholic, I tried to resist most things Father Njhay said. But I wanted to take this one on board, especially now, as I looked at that weather beaten face in the mirror. I went back into the cafe.

"You look ok," Arthur said.

"I feel ok," I told him.

Not long after, campaigning began for the mayoral elections in Santa Fe. Our dear friend Di was up against a woman by the name of Emily Janeway. Emily was young and pretty and blonde and married to one of the wealthiest men in New Mexico. So she had the financial support, and the look, and she took that look all around the town, on television, and to any number of functions for key voters and lobbyists.

Now Emily was, not surprisingly, opposed to everything the Mayor stood for. But it was the way she was opposed that was just a little frightening. She somehow managed to make all the mayor's policies seem un-American, subversive and something to be feared. She traded in a language reminiscent of an oil billionaire and politician well-known to her husband, where everyone that wasn't with her was against her.

The really frightening thing was that, whereas there were any number of issues which could have been the focus of the campaign, the one that seemed to galvanize everyone, was us. I still don't quite understand it, but somehow we became the symbol both sides seized on, for better or for worse.

For the Janeway camp we represented everything Santa Fe needed to fight against. We were undignified. We were loose cannon. We stood for a radical element which just took over the city, terrorized the locals, and drove them and the honest tourist out of the town center with our bawdiness and our boisterousness. We were cross dressers (I was still playing Blanche), we were gay, and we were 'actors'. Worst of all, one of us was a foreigner. Indeed it was often said I was an 'illegal'. This despite my having a green card, and having lived and worked in the U.S.A most of my adult life.

What's more the city was paying us with

'unauthorized' funds to spoil the peace in the Old Town Square, and letting us live rent free in a condemned city property.

Soon we found supporters of both camps turning up to our performances, the Janewayites jeering us and the mayor's supporters cheering us. Needless to say no-one heard a word we said. We had stopped being a theater troupe and had become a focal point for fierce verbal clashes between the factions.

One day those clashes went beyond the verbal and erupted into a full scale brawl, right in the middle of the balcony scene from Romeo and Juliet. Arthur and I tried to reason with the Montagues and the Capulets. We tried to explain we were no risk to anyone. The result was a broken toe for Arthur and three missing teeth for me.

I would like to say the mayor trounced this troublemaker in the election. But Emily Janeway was the clear winner. Her inauguration of course meant the end of the semi-official promenade street theater troupe of Santa Fe.

In the midst of her disappointment, the ex-Mayor still managed to seek us out and commiserate with us.

"I'm ashamed this all happened," she said. "Politics can be a cruel business."

"And a little distorting," Arthur smiled. "Here we are, two heterosexual men, pure capitalists, running our little business, making our profits whilst at the same time garnering support from the public purse, and failing to pay taxes. But we are accused of being gay communist illegals, and are run out of town."

"You deserve better," Di said. "And maybe you'll get better."

She handed us a card. It bore the name 'Ambrose Slattery, Mayor of the City of Las Vegas'.

"He's a good friend," Di told us. "A political brother. I've taken the liberty of approaching him on your behalf. He's all for having you in Vegas. A bit of a loose cannon, just like you guys. You'll be amazed what he comes up with."

We told our benefactor just how grateful we were. The semi-official promenade street theater troupe of Arthur and Joe couldn't wait to promenade on the famous Vegas strip.

"Why don't you come with us, Di?" Arthur suggested. "It would be great to have a real woman playing Blanche and Juliet."

"Thanks, boys," she said, laughing. "But politicians make bad actors, just as actors make bad politicians. Besides I have to stay here and prepare for the next election."

14.

We never did meet Ambrose Slattery. But we didn't mind. The Mayor of Las Vegas was a busy man. We understood that. What's more he sent a stream of assistants to make sure we were taken care of, each younger and prettier than the last. We didn't really mind that either. It had been a long time since either Arthur or I had kept company with a young, sane and attractive woman.

The first, whose name I think was Jazz, or maybe Jatz, told us that she was a city employee by day, and a dancer by night. She, like the Mayor, was also busy.

"The Mayor has arranged accommodation for you," she told us.

We expected to be driven way out into the suburbs or even to a shack in the desert. Instead she took us to a penthouse at the Bellagio. She explained this was where 'extinguished' guests of the city stayed, but that they weren't expecting any for some time. Then she looked embarrassed and said:

"Not that you're not extinguished. I just..."

"Don't worry," Arthur laughed.

"It's just there is one tiny condition." She looked abashed.

"Whatever it is, we don't mind," I told her.

"It's just that if extinguished guests do arrive, um, er, I mean other extinguished guests...."

"You want us to vacate," Arthur said.

"Yes, that's it." She looked relieved.

That settled, Jazz/Jatz then took us on a tour of the apartment. There were two bedrooms, each with a bed about as wide as the whole portico at Sts Peter and Paul. We had two bathrooms each (a his and a hers). Each bathroom had a daunting control panel on the wall.

"I don't really know what all those switches do," Jatz confessed, at which point Arthur started playing with them. He soon had the shower running from both overhead and side jets, the mood music playing, the radio on, the flat screen TV pumping at full volume, and a range of lights doing a range of things in sequence. It was a bit like a fun parlor and just as tiring, till we got everything under control.

We also had a dining room and a sitting room, as well as a kitchen, a 'nook' with a roll top desk and writing implements, and a powder room. All up we counted seven flat screen TVs, one in each bedroom, one in each of the four bathrooms, and a giant one in the sitting room. After Jazz had gone we turned them all on at once, just to see what it felt like, and spent the next hour wandering about the penthouse playing with all the toys.

Jatz had told us room service was at our disposal, but the Mayor would appreciate it if we didn't exceed $200 dollars per day. We thought that was fine too. Of course we ordered immediately. As we sat at our dining table in our penthouse on the 36th floor of the Bellagio, eating our club sandwiches and sipping our New Zealand sauvignon blanc, looking out over the Bellagio fountain, the Paris, the suburbs of Vegas and on to the desert beyond, it occurred to us that maybe our luck had changed.

In fact every time things had gone really wrong of late, they had led to something so much better. We had been so sad to leave Boulder and the disciples, but had ended up with a great life in Santa Fe. Now after being run out of that town, we were high above the city of dreams, with all our needs catered for. It seemed almost wrong somehow.

I can't really explain why I felt that way. When I had been wealthy and part of the Vanderveer Empire, nothing could have seemed more natural. But when you have hit the bottom, and risen again, you wonder how long it will last. The illusion of security has no place in your psyche any more. Besides, you can't help thinking about those who haven't risen up with you. I asked Arthur if he thought the disciples were all right. It was something I had asked many times before. I got the same answer as before:

"I like to say I'm sure of it," he said. "But..."

We were silent for a while then. I was thinking back to all that had happened since Father Njhay had been taken out of our lives. I guess Arthur was doing much the same. Our reverie was finally broken by the arrival of another of the Mayor's staff, a young woman named Deneice (yes pronounced just like Denise), who was also a dancer by night. Her job was to show us where we were to perform.

We were given a range of options along and behind the strip and were told we could move from one to the other whenever we liked, so long as we did four shows per day. We were very happy with that. In the end we decided to concentrate on the pedestrian walkways, footbridges and open area, back from the strip, which linked the Bellagio to Caesar's Palace, and the strip itself right in front of the Bellagio fountain.

We injected our Vegas shows with much more contemporary material. For some reason we used a lot of Paul Simon's lyrics, and called our show *The Human Zoo* because someone told us it was all happening at the zoo.

We were rocks, we were islands, and we were bridges over troubled waters, especially on the pedestrian bridge between Caesar's and the Bellagio. We threw off that hazy shade of winter, and burst forth into a Las Vegas summer.

We had a lot of fun doing Paul Simon, and Van Morrison, and Henry Lawson and scenes from *Friends*. Arthur did an uncanny Chandler, and it was my delight to play the Filipino houseboy:

"More turkey Mr Chandler?"

There really was no logic to our shows. There were no themes other than the theme of raw fun. We did what we pleased and the surging mass of the Vegas audience seemed happy. In fact the Bellagio management asked the Mayor if we could do some of our show in and around the hotel.

Of course our apartment was so big we could use it as a rehearsal studio. There we contrived our characters and our scenes. But our best trick was because of the Bellagio fountain. We realized the fountain came on with such precision we could literally set our watches by it.

Knowing exactly when that massive burst of Vegas energy would set off, gave us our ultimate party trick. We did Macbeth's soliloquy timed to finish just before the fountain exploded. So we would be down on the Strip in front of the fountain and we would end with:

> "It is a tale told by an idiot
> Full of sound and fury
> Signifying NOTHING!"

And as we bellowed NOTHING in unison, the very opposite of nothing would happen, for the fountain behind us would burst into action. It was a crowd pleaser all right, we with our hands to the heavens, the water seeming to spurt from our very fingertips.

Sometimes admittedly we got the timing slightly wrong, and when we yelled NOTHING, there was indeed nothing. But then we would just yell NOTHING a few more times, as if for emphasis, and eventually the fountain would oblige. We felt the audience were completely fooled. After all how could they know how many 'nothings' were in the script.

However an audience has a habit of keeping

you honest. One night a young boy, probably not more than seven, came up to us after the show and said:

"Last night you got the fountain to work on the first 'nothing'. How come you needed three 'nothings' tonight?"

"Sometimes the fountain gets stubborn," Arthur told him, at which he ran back to his parents, yelling:

"It's a stubborn fountain."

15.

We had been playing Vegas like this for about six months, and by some miracle, still no 'extinguished' guests had arrived to eject us from our penthouse.

We were doing a show one night down in front of the fountain, and were just about to launch into the Macbeth finale, when Arthur whispered to me:

"Isn't that Max Broun?"

I looked up, and yes it did look very much like the man who was one of the richest men in America. His crumpled face and avuncular demeanor were well known to just about everyone in the U.S.A. I watched as he turned to say something to his companion.

She looked familiar too. In fact she was *very*

familiar. I felt a surge of delight pass over me, for it was Marjorie. I turned to Arthur:

"That's Pete Vanderveer's mother," I told him. "With Broun. It's Marjorie Vanderveer,"

"And Pete himself, if I'm not mistaken. Not to mention your Katherine."

"What?!"

I turned back and saw it was true. All in a line next to Broun. Marjorie and Pete and Katherine, all smiling at me like a row of cheshire cats. I'm not sure if I smiled back, because now Arthur was nudging me and showing me his watch. We were already past the start time for the soliloquy.

We launched into our act, picking up the tempo to try and compensate for the lost time. But we were hopelessly out of sync and the fountain beat us to the punch. The waters of the Bellagio washed over the last two lines of our finale.

Then Marjorie and Katherine were hugging me and making a lot of incoherent noises. I was conscious of Pete standing right by, and thought he might hug me too. But it was not our way. So when Marjorie and Katherine had finished he took my hand and almost shook it off.

It felt wonderful. I hadn't realized just how much I'd missed them. Everyone was talking at once as we were introducing Arthur and Max Broun and at the same time trying to explain what we had all been doing over the last couple of years.

Of course I knew what they had been doing.

They were celebrities. I had seen them on TV. They were doing things no-one had done before. Philanthropic celebrities. It was wonderful, I told them. I was proud of them all, I said, and I meant it. But what I had done was a little more difficult to explain. I'm sure I made no sense at all. Finally Max Broun said we should all slow down and he took us for cocktails at the Rhumbar outside the Mirage.

Katherine sat next to me, and of course all the old feelings were still there. I guess I wasn't surprised. But a part of me had hoped one day I would be able to see her again, and it would be different. A part of me hoped my feelings would catch up with the reality of life. But it was not to be.

After we had had a couple of drinks, Katherine leaned across to me and said:

"Why did you leave us, Joe? It was hard for us, never to hear from you, not knowing where you were. It was like someone just cut off an arm. You must have known that."

"I thought it might be a little difficult for you, for a while," I confessed.

"A little difficult? Now there's an understatement."

She sounded quite distressed, and I felt bad. I had never guessed they would feel as strongly as they did. I apologized but it seemed woefully inadequate.

"Why did you do it?" she repeated. "I've

thought about it a thousand times. I've talked to Marjorie and Pete about it a thousand times too. We think we know but I need to hear it from you."

And now here we were again. The chasm of miscommunication across which I could not jump. Did they know the truth and just wanted to have it confirmed? Or did they have the whole thing wrong? Then what if I surprised Katherine with the real truth? Where would that leave us? Either way I could see no point inserting my pain between her and Pete. What would it serve? In the end, weakly, I just said:

"I just can't talk about it. I couldn't talk about it then, and I can't now. Nothing has changed."

"OK, Joe," she sighed. "As you wish."

A little later Pete sat down on the other side of me.

"I was really angry with you," he said.

"I guessed you might be."

"But I'm not anymore. I was just so excited when I saw you. If there was any anger left, *The Human Zoo* got rid of it."

"You liked my acting?"

"Arthur was the star," he smiled. "But you weren't bad as Lady Macbeth."

"All my best roles are females. I'm not sure what that tells us."

"I'm not sure either. Probably not much." He looked at me for a long moment, obviously trying to decide something. In the end he just said: "I think I know why you did it. But I'm not going to ask. I'm sure it was a decision not easily taken."

"The hardest decision of my life," I told him.

"We've kept your money aside. Just in case"

"What money?" I had actually forgotten I had given them all my money. It seemed so long ago, and in a life belonging to someone else.

"The money you gave the Foundation. We kept it aside. Just in case we found you again. Just in case you needed it."

I laughed then, as so many moments of need flashed through my mind. But I said:

"I gave it to the Foundation, because the Foundation was doing such a great job. I want the Foundation to have it."

"Is that true, Joe? Do you really believe we are doing the right thing?"

"Of course. I said so earlier tonight. I am so proud of you. You are doing something no-one has done. You are making your philanthropy the center of the game. It's amazing."

"Yes you did say that." He was very serious now. "But I thought maybe that was for Arthur's benefit, or Max's."

"Why would I need to bother?"

"I guess you wouldn't."

Pete hung his head and was silent for a long time. When he looked up, his eyes were those of a little boy wanting approval.

"It's just...you loved Marcellus, and you trusted his vision, and I have strayed so far from it."

I couldn't believe what I was hearing.

"I told you long ago, if Marcellus had seen what you had seen, he would have approved of what you are doing, completely. Don't you remember?"

"Yes, Joe, I remember you said that. But I thought maybe I had gone too far, way too far, in your eyes."

Then it struck me.

"Is that why you think I left? You think I disapproved, and so I left?"

"Yes, that's what we thought. We couldn't image what else would make you go like that."

"Can't you? Can't you really?"

"No!" he said, and it was perfectly clear he had no idea.

"When I wrote my letter of resignation, I said that I blessed the work you were doing."

"Yes I know, but even so."

"Even so what?"

"We thought maybe...on one level you were happy for us to do what made us happy...but on another you couldn't be part of it."

It was an amazing lesson for me, in just how differently people will see a situation, how very far apart their interpretations can be. It was also a lesson about never making an assumption. If you want to cut up your credit cards and give your money away and become a hobo, don't assume everyone is going to understand why.

"I approve, totally, on every level," I told him.

"And I was proud of the small part I played in it, before I left."

"Then why?" He was almost beseeching me. "Why did you go?"

I just didn't answer. I didn't know how. So Pete, reluctantly, let it go. And I was very glad I hadn't told Katherine the truth.

"If you like what we're doing, and you liked your part in it," he said at length, "then come back and be a part of it again. Please, Joe."

It broke my heart the way he said that. This man loved me. And I realized, for the first time, he looked up to me. Perhaps because I had been anointed by Marcellus. Till now the idea had never crossed my mind.

"Thank you," I said. "But I have another life now. Arthur depends on me for all those female roles. Besides, the reason I left is still with me. I know it seems petulant not to want to talk about it. But I just can't. And while it's with me, I don't see myself being any use to you."

"I know that's just not true. Listen, Joe, we're here with Max to do some business, a sort of working holiday. But really I want to try and get him to support the Foundation. I think I can. At least I hope so. If you would help, I just know we'd succeed."

"I think you overestimate my abilities," I smiled.

"I don't. I know you'd win him round." He paused again. I could see him trying to decide whether to play his ace. "You ran out on us, Joe. And you won't even tell me why. OK, that's your choice. But I think you owe me one."

"I guess maybe I do," I had to admit.

"Then come with us tomorrow. We're all going for a boat ride on Lake Mead. Come with us. See what you can do with Broun. If you don't get anywhere and you really want to go back to your street theater, I won't try to stop you."

"Can I bring Arthur?" I smiled.

"Of course you can bring Arthur."

I really doubted I would have any sway over a man like Broun. But I did owe it to Pete to give it a go, if that's what he wanted. His Marcellus substitute had let him down badly. He could at least try to make amends. Little was I to know how successful I would be, and why.

16.

Next day we drove out to Lake Mead together. A big beautiful two storey houseboat was waiting for us, fully stocked and catered. We motored right out into the lake. Liveried waiters brought round plates of food and champagne. It was a beautiful sunny day. Arthur was having a wonderful time, and was keeping Katherine and Marjorie amused with tales of his Chicago theater days and of our days as the Arthur and Joe semi-official promenade theater troupe.

I was standing alone on the upper deck watching the speed boats cut across the lake, and wondering how I would approach Max Broun, when he solved the problem for me, by coming up the stairs and saying:

"I've heard a lot about you from Pete and Katherine."

"We go back a long way."

"Bit of mystery why you disappeared on them." Then he smiled a kind of knowing smile, and added: "Or it is for them anyway."

"You've got it worked out, have you?" I asked.

"Well, I'm only guessing, but I think maybe you had to leave something or someone behind."

"Is that your guess?" I smiled.

"It is." He smiled back. "I think maybe you have a thing for Katherine. I see the way you look at her.'

I was amazed, but said only:

"I never look at her."

"That's my point. It's unnatural."

He laughed then, and I couldn't help laughing too. I suppose a man doesn't get that rich without being a sharp observer of people.

"They're keen to get you involved in the Foundation," I said. There seemed little point in subtleties with a man like this.

"Yes I know."

"And they think I'll be able to talk you

round."

"I realize that too. That's why I came up here. To give you a chance to talk me round."

He sat down, propped on the railing of the upper deck, with his back to the water, and took a long sip of his champagne.

"I have a feeling a man like you only gets talked round when he wants to get talked round."

"Probably true," he said. "But I'm inclined towards what they're doing. Perhaps not in the big way they hope. But I'm inclined nonetheless."

"That's good," I said. As he had been talking I had been half conscious of a motor boat cutting through the water near where we were, doubling back on itself, going way to fast and way to close to us. "So let's just think about...", I started, but again the motor boat caught my attention as it shot by our houseboat.

Then before I knew it, and before I could speak again, the boat had circled to the opposite side from us. It must have lost control for it ploughed into the other side of the houseboat. It hit with a thud. The houseboat shuddered, and Max Broun ever so delicately tipped backwards off the railing where he was perched, and into the water. I rushed to the railing, saw him hit the water and go straight down. He didn't come back up.

I was a lifeguard, a Bra Boy. I didn't think twice. I climbed up on the railing, noted the ripples where he had entered and dove for them.

The water was clear and as I opened my eyes I could see him. But he was going down fast, feet first, seeming to make no attempt to save himself. I had to work hard to get to him.

I got behind, put my palm under his chin, and started kicking for the surface. When we finally got there I had little breath left and Max was unconscious. I screamed to the others to help, and soon we had him on the deck. I did CPR, Max vomited and regained consciousness, and not long after we had a water ambulance to take him to the hospital in Vegas.

I visited him that night. He was sitting up in bed reading the financial papers. He smiled when he saw me.

"I can't swim," he said.

"I guessed that," I replied.

"Thank you," he said, quite simply, and his eyes told me just how grateful he was.

We made small talk for a while after that, when out of nowhere Max laughed and said:

"Bet you think you'll get me to contribute to the Foundation now."

"The thought never crossed my mind."

"Well I will." He was now quite serious. "Of course I will. I thought I was gone, but you saved me. It makes you think. When you come close to death, it makes you think. It's a cliché but it's true."

I felt strangely embarrassed by this. I did what I had done by instinct. I didn't want him feeling beholden to me or to any cause he felt I was pushing. And that's what I told him.

"Still, I *will* get involved. I think it's meant to be. The only question is, how will I get involved, and how much? And that depends on what I decide about a few things. Listen, Joe, I'll be out of here tomorrow. Is there somewhere we can meet with the Vanderveers tomorrow night? Somewhere we can all talk, in comfort? I reckon I'll have it worked out by then"

"Arthur and I have a penthouse at the Bellagio," I told him.

"No kidding!"

"No kidding. Street theater pays well in Vegas."

"Ok," he laughed. 'See you at your penthouse at eight."

That night everyone was early and we sat waiting for Max to arrive. I looked at the faces of the people I loved and saw them filled with anticipation. For Pete and Katherine, and Marjorie too, it was about how much Max would give, how far he would commit himself. It was potentially the biggest step forward yet for the Foundation. Arthur's eyes were full of anticipation too. For him it was about the theater of life. He couldn't wait to see how this drama would unfold.

For my part I felt flat. I wanted to share in their excitement, but something was holding me back. Maybe it was, as always, the way I felt about Katherine. That emotion just seemed to stand between me and any other emotion I might feel, blocking the other, making the other less relevant, maybe even not relevant at all. Or perhaps I was just so embarrassed at the fuss everyone was making about my saving Max. I just didn't know.

When the guest of honor arrived he got straight to the point. He sat us all down on a ring of huge Bellagio armchairs and couches, whilst he stood before us ready to bestow his bounty on us, or his wisdom, or both.

I had a flash of when Marcellus was dying, and he lined up Marjorie and Pete and I on the couch whilst he stood with his back to the fire. It was totally different of course; different scenario, different locale, even some different players. But what it had in common with that earlier moment was its potential, one man's potential, to change so many lives.

"I'm nearly 70 years old," Max said. "Yesterday I was very close to death. I said to Joe that it makes you think. It does. It made me think. I've been a businessman all my life, and I have been very good at the business of business. I have accumulated lots of money and lots of things. I have more than I could ever use, or any of those dependent on me could ever use. I give to charity. I give big time. $200 million per year. People say I'm generous. I guess I am. Lots of people benefit. But I always think – what have I changed? Is the world any different?"

We all just sat there listening. There was no

way anyone was going to speak. He continued:

"But you guys, you are seriously at risk of changing the world. Everyone is saying so, and they are right. Why? Because you have taken philanthropy out of the realm of the amateur and made it your core business. We've all thought, at one time or another, how great that would be. But we've always believed it was one or the other. Either run your business and give a little away, or give it all away and go out of business. But you have shown how the business of business and," he was searching for the right words, "the business of love can work in tandem, to the benefit of both."

It was a beautiful thing to say, a wonderful way to describe it – the business of love. I felt a lump the size of a tennis ball in my throat.

"And I want to be a part of it," Max was continuing. "I want to do what you are doing, and preferably *with* you, if you'll have me."

Everyone was still silent. Did he want Pete or Katherine to respond? I didn't know. In the end they said nothing and Max continued:

"I've done a lot of thinking in the last 24 hours, and I know what I want to do and how I want to do it. Getting near death clears the mind, doesn't it Joe?"

I wondered if he was referring to Katherine saving my life.

"I *have* been close to death," I said.

"I know. It was her saving you, and the need you felt to give back, which started everything

Pete and Katherine are doing. Is it karma? Is that what they call it? Now you save me. Now I want to give back too."

I was amazed how much Max knew about me. Luckily he didn't seem to know the mixed motives which drove me to give away that first million dollars of Pete's money. He was looking directly at me. A response was definitely needed.

"Getting near death certainly helps you know what you want," I said, remembering, in the midst of the gun battle, how I thought more of Katherine than the risk to my own life.

"That's it exactly," Max said. "I now know what I want. I'm surprised I didn't know it before. But at least I know it now, thanks to Joe."

"Thanks to Joe," Marjorie said very softly. Then, a little louder to Max: "Tell us what it is you *do* want, Max."

"I want to give the Foundation $5 billion per year. That is a minimum. Depending on how things go, I may be able to give more. But I know I can give $5 billion without risk, so I'll say that. Then you have a bottom line to work with."

"Wow!" Arthur couldn't help saying.

"That is very generous," said Pete, and we could see he was totally astonished. We all were. Nobody had expected anything like that. "Let me just say…"

"Wait," said Max interrupting. "I have conditions. You may not like them. Don't thank me yet."

"All right," said Pete. "What are the conditions?"

"First of all I want a seat on the Board of the Foundation. An equal partner with you. Three directors. Pete and Katherine and Max."

Pete turned to Katherine who shrugged and smiled. Pete smiled too. We all did, at the audacity of it, at the grandeur of the whole thing.

"Done!" Pete said.

Now it was Max's turn to smile.

"Second condition is we set up a dedicated subsidiary company. Dedicated to the sole task of getting people like me on board. The real brilliance of your work is what Katherine has always understood. Take the revenue of the world's largest companies, divide it by the cost of ending hunger and poverty, and the profits will still be more than enough to keep all the shareholders happy. What's more you've just created a whole new market of healthy people with the money to buy your products. It's irrefutable logic."

"It certainly is," said Marjorie, with pride in her voice. Katherine looked down at the ground, but I saw a tiny smile come into the corner of her mouth.

"But you need to get those companies committed," Max continued, "or rather their controlling minds. You need to get the others on board, or some of them. Enough of them. I know that's what you're trying to do. But you're doing it piecemeal. You have to make that aspect of your business as efficient and as business-like as the rest."

"Also irrefutable logic," Marjorie said.

"Yes," Pete added, "You're right. We'll do that."

Max smiled. Then he said: "So that leaves condition 3." He looked about him and it seemed this was the one he was most looking forward to. "We have to get the right person to head up the subsidiary. For me there is only one choice, and you all know who that is."

"Ah!" they all said at once, turning to me.

"If you don't take it, Joe, the deal is off," Max said.

I laughed but no-one else did.

"I'm serious," Max said. "If you don't take the job, it's a deal breaker."

I looked at him for a moment, trying to work out just how serious he was. I couldn't tell. In the end I said:

"Max, any one of a thousand people could do that job."

"I don't agree," he said. "Take me for example. The world sees me as a tough character. The world sees me as someone not so easy to bring round. But you got me. You brought me round big time."

"Yes but I can't go saving the lives of every billionaire on the planet."

"You'll do what you need to do. Maybe it

won't *always* be saving their lives," he smiled, "but you'll convince them one way or another."

"For a start," Pete said, 'you'll tell them how it changed me, and how *that* made me want to change the suffering I saw about me."

"That's it," said Max, 'You'll tell them that. You'll make them understand because you believe in what Pete and Katherine are doing."

"I do believe it," I couldn't help admitting. "But..."

"But you have reasons why you left," said Max, "and the reasons are still there."

"Yes," I said, feeling rather foolish, and hanging my head.

Max came over to me now, and put his hand on my shoulder. He said very gently:

"Well, get past them, will you, Joe? For all our sakes."

"Please, Joe," Pete said.

"Please," Katherine echoed.

I looked over at Arthur who was smiling at me. His eyes told me to go for it. Then I looked at Marjorie. She said:

"I think you want everyone to go now, don't you, Joe? So you have some time to think this over."

"Yes," I said, grateful to her. "That would be good."

As they all filed out, Marjorie hung back and said:

"Do you want me to stay for a while?"

"Yes, I really do," I smiled.

So the others left and Marjorie sat back down on one of the big couches. Arthur asked if he should leave the room, but Marjorie told him to stay. I poured us all a drink. I heard myself sigh deeply as I sank down into one of the armchairs. We were silent together for a little while until finally Marjorie spoke:

"Pete and Katherine think you left because you didn't approve of their philanthropy, or at least the level of their philanthropy."

"Why would they think that?" Arthur asked.

"Because people can't live with no answer. If they haven't got a good one, they'll tend to assign a bad one, rather than leave themselves wondering," Marjorie said.

"Anyway, I set them straight," I said.

"Yes but did you tell them the real reason?" Marjorie asked. "Did you tell them it was because you love Katherine and you can't bear to be around her when you can't have her?"

"You're smart," Arthur smiled.

Marjorie smiled back at him but said nothing. She was waiting for me to speak.

"How could I tell them that?" I said, hearing a raspy tone in my voice I didn't like. "What would it achieve?"

"It would only make them uncomfortable, to say the least" Marjorie replied.

It felt good to have someone else name my problem, though of course it went no way to solving it.'

"So of course I can't just go back to that. Nothing has changed," I said.

"Are you sure?" Arthur surprised me by saying.

"Yes," Marjorie said. "Are you sure. Because, you know Joe, something *has* changed." I just looked at her, so she continued: "Pete and Katherine, and now Max, are carrying the ball down field, and they want to pass it to you to make the touchdown."

"In rugby we call it a 'try', not a touchdown. I never got a try for the Galloping Greens. Katherine's brother got several on the other wing, but my only one was disallowed."

I was mumbling to myself really, making noise to try and make sense of how I was feeling.

"I'm not really sure what you just said," she told me, "but it sounds like you might be getting ready to take that pass."

"I don't know if I have the strength," I said.

"You'll be going round the world all the time. You'll hardly ever see her," Marjorie said. "But the bottom line is this: whatever pain you get from being near Katherine, I think it's a pain worth enduring. I know that's easy for me to say. But I think it's true. How many people get a chance to help change the world?"

She was looking at me now, her eyes bright.

"Probably not many," those eyes forced me to confess.

"Besides," she added, "you won't be alone. I'll be there to dry your tears. And you'll have Arthur too."

"Will I?"

"Will he?" Arthur was astonished.

"Of course. It would be a shame to break up the semi-official promenade theater troupe. We just have to make the promenade longer."

"Would they really let me take Arthur?"

"They'll let you do whatever you want."

"Would you come?" I asked Arthur. "I think if you were there maybe I could do it."

"Would I get a big office?" he asked, laughing.

"Overlooking the Avenue of the Americas," Marjorie said.

I felt a huge smile cover my face.

"Just one tiny detail," Marjorie laughed. "If you're going to smile that broadly, you'll need three false teeth. Or two for an ordinary grin."

"I'll get all three," I re-assured her.

So then Arthur and I gave our notice to the Mayor, or at least to one of his attractive assistants, and relinquished our penthouse, for a less opulent, but nonetheless more than satisfactory (as far as Arthur was concerned) couple of adjoining offices overlooking the Avenue of the Americas.

17.

On our first morning we had a visit from Max Broun. We had been sitting in my office looking down on the street, trying to find a way to start. We had been carried back to New York, to this new adventure, on the wave of everyone's enthusiasm. But now we were here, it was all starting to look a bit tough. Then, all of a sudden, Max just strolled in, unannounced, looking fit and ready for action.

"I've just got you a walk up start," he said. "Jeremiah Janeway is on board. Old friend of mine. Just a small kick of the can, but he's in, and you can work on him over time."

"Isn't he...?" I began.

"Yes, the husband of the mayor who ran you out of Santa Fe." Once again Max was fully informed. "But he never listens to his wife. Fortunately! Here's his pledge."

Max threw a piece of paper on my desk, and was gone as quickly as he had appeared. We heard him chuckling to himself down the corridor.

"He loves life." Arthur said.

"Good thing I saved it then."

"Maybe we could just do nothing, and leave it to Max."

"It's as good a plan as any we have at the moment," I felt constrained to admit. But Arthur had been thinking.

"Perhaps we've already done the groundwork," he said.

"My new teeth?"

"Well yes that, but also the Arthur and Joe semi-official promenade theater troupe."

"We're going to perform for the world's billionaires?"

"Not exactly. But after a fashion. You remember when I was training you as an actor? What was the number one thing I stressed?"

"Belief?"

"Yes belief. And why?"

"Because if you believe, you will be honest."

"Correct. And if you are honest?"

"Then the audience will believe too. The audience will care."

"Again correct. Now with a fictional character it's hard to find that belief. We have to pull in a backstory, find an emotion memory, and use our imagination. But with you, Joe Starling, the real Joe Starling playing himself – the belief is already there."

"Is it there for the real Arthur T. Arthurson?" I asked, but I knew the answer.

"Yes it is," he assured me. "I want to be part of this adventure too. It's a truly great gig."

"So what you're saying is that the semi-official promenade theater troupe will just go about the world performing all the wonderful possibilities this has to offer, both for the givers, and for those to whom they give."

"Or in other words," he said, smiling, "we'll give it to them straight. Our costumes will be our own suits, our dialogue will be our own words, and the power of our performance will be our own belief."

"Thanks Arthur," I said, and I felt myself break into a huge smile.

Just then Marjorie walked by my office.

"Good job," she said.

"What?"

"The teeth!" And she was gone down the corridor.

So Arthur and I got ourselves the Bloomberg Top 200 Billionaires List and started to plan our attack. But that night I couldn't sleep. Something was still wrong. No matter how much I believed myself, no matter how charismatic the semi-official promenade theater troupe might be, I just couldn't see any of those tough, successful people, being convinced to hand over their money. Next morning I called a meeting in my office.

"Look, Max," I said. "You might be able to get Jeremiah Janeway to hand over his money just like that. But you know him, he's an old friend. How will I manage to convince total strangers, who by the way didn't get where they are by being pushovers, to just give the Foundation their money?"

"You won't," said Max. "Is that what you thought your job was?"

"That's what I thought his job was," Pete said.

Marjorie and Katherine nodded. Max shook his head.

"Janeway gave us some pennies, "Max said. "Others may too, if you ask. But we want the sort of commitment from them that Pete and Katherine are making. Your job, Joe, is to convince them, in the context of their own businesses, to take the business of giving, and make it the center of their game."

"But then we would have no control over what sort of things they do," said Pete.

"Of course not," said Max. "What right would we have to dictate to them anyway? Would you like it if they tried to tell us what to do? The genius of these people is their individuality and their entrepreneurship. That's what Joe and Arthur have to encourage. They have to say: 'Look what fun Pete and Katherine are having. Look how happy Max is.' Then leave them alone. They'll take the same genius and drive that made them rich, and they'll use it to cure whatever they choose to cure. And they'll have a great time along the way."

There was no doubt Max was right, but Pete said:

"Let's suppose we're successful and create a world of rich men and women all doing their own thing. Wouldn't there be overlap, inevitably, with several people working on the same problem and other problems going unsolved."

"Certainly, for a time," Max said. "But better

to have two lots of ten billion dollars overlapping on the elimination of AIDS in Africa, than two lots of a million dollars going into our cheque account. Anyway they'll sort it out. The wealthy specialize in carving up markets and eliminating competition. That's the key to their success."

"Nice to have you on the team," Katherine said.

18.

After that Arthur and I were ready to go. As Arthur put it, the gig had been re-defined, and the audience demographic had been clarified. The question was where to start. We knew how important our first approach would be. If we got that right, others might follow. I had two candidates in mind, both Australians.

The first was a man who'd made his fortune in the unlikely combination of gold mining and brewing. He lived in Australia, regularly commuting between the outback and Sydney. His name was also an unlikely combination – Forrest Woodland. But for Arthur T. Arthurson and Joe Stalin, that could only be a plus.

Another plus was that Woodland had already done some great work employing underprivileged Aboriginal people in his mining operations. So we thought he might be receptive to our message.

The other Australian was a media magnate who lived in the States. John Stockton, was more generally known as Stinky. He was by far the richer of the two, and was a lot closer to home. But his philanthropic philosophy was unknown. And if his nickname was anything to go by...

While we were discussing the pros and cons of our first contact, Pete came into my office.

"My instincts tell me to go with Woodland," he said.

That was a wonderful thing for me to hear, from the man who once told his father he didn't think he *had* instincts. I must have been looking at him for too long, because he said:

"You don't agree?"

I felt myself smile and say: "Oh yes, I agree totally."

Clearly Pete did not remember what he had told his father. It was lost in the joys of his new found self. That made me very happy.

So in deference to Pete's instincts, we made contact with Woodland and took a flight out to Sydney. He had asked that we meet in the bar of the Frisco Hotel in Woolloomooloo. As Arthur and I stood on the corner of Bland St and Cowper Wharf Road, next to the 1840s terrace houses, looking out over the glistening waters of Sydney Harbour on that perfectly clear summer's day, I was reminded what a beautiful city I had grown up in.

We turned to enter the pub, but found that

Woodland was right behind us. He had obviously been standing watching us for some time.

"Everyone looks in that direction," he said, a broad smile on his face. He was tall and sunburnt and wore shorts, sandals and an Akubra hat. He looked like he had taken one giant stride from The Kimberley to be here.

"It's a nice view," Arthur said.

"Physically beautiful *and* opulent," Woodland said. "See there," pointing to the Woolloomooloo Finger Wharf. "One of the most sought after pieces of real estate in Australia. All the big shots stay at The Blue, and all the stars have an apartment there. I'm right next to Russell Crowe."

But he wasn't boasting. His words were delivered just as a matter of fact.

"I'm Joe Starling," I said, holding out my hand.

"Of course you are," he said, shaking it vigorously. "And you're Arthur, the thespian. How's Pete? Met him once. Shy little bugger. Don't know how he does everything he does, when he's that shy."

He spoke very fast.

"He's not so shy anymore," I said.

"How did you know I was an actor?" Arthur asked.

"Knowledge is power," Woodland smiled again. "I also know you were both hobos. That is bloody fantastic!" He threw his head back and laughed. "Here you are, given the job of chatting up billionaires and just a few months ago you were bums." He laughed again.

Arthur and I didn't know whether to be embarrassed or amused.

"That's why I wanted to meet you here," he continued. "I wanted you to stand right here looking two hundred yards in that direction to some of the greatest wealth in this nation, and then show you, two hundred yards in the other direction, some of the worst poverty. I knew you guys would appreciate that, being bums and all." He chuckled and corrected himself: "Ex-bums I mean. No offence."

"None taken," we both assured him at once.

"Come with me," he said, and we followed as he led the way up Dowling Street, away from the Harbour.

Sure enough, about two hundred yards up the hill we came upon a bunch of homeless men sitting on benches just across from The Old Fitzroy Hotel. Woodland strode up to them and shook the hand of one of the older men, if anything more vigorously than he had shaken mine.

"This is Manny," he told us. "Manny has the distinction of being both an alcoholic and a schizophrenic. Isn't that right Manny?"

"I'm afraid so," Manny replied.

"But we're going to fix all that, aren't we, Manny?"

"Yes, Forrest," he replied, but looked far from convinced.

Forrest sat us down next to Manny on the bench amongst the homeless men.

"The way I plan to do it," he started to explain, "is a little ironic. I'm going to take all the alcoholics (and the others of course) and get them working in my brewery." He laughed.

Manny, who couldn't help overhearing, because Forrest Woodland didn't just speak fast, but also loudly, looked both dubious and excited at the same time.

"See that's what I've done up in the Kimberley and in the Territory. I've taken these Aborigines off the missions. Everyone says they're hopeless, but I've given them jobs in the mines. They're not hopeless. Of course they're not." As he got more excited, his speech got faster and louder. "They work the heavy machinery like they were weaving baskets. Like craftsmen, like poets they are. They take all that ancient wisdom and apply it to something altogether new. That's what I call flexible."

"You obviously admire them," Arthur said.

"Not all of them," Forrest smiled. "Some of those bastards are just as lazy as our lazy bastards." He hesitated for a moment, then spoke a good deal more seriously. "But yes, I admire the way most go about their lives. And they've made my life a lot easier."

"When I was growing up I remember quite a different attitude from miners and pastoralists," I said.

"Well, maybe I'm part of a new breed," Forrest replied with a determination in his voice. "I hope I'm a bit like Pete. I hope, in my own small way, I can emulate him. I want to make this stuff the center of my business." Then he stopped and smiled again, saying: "So I'm sorry if you boys made this long trip for nothing. You came to talk me into something I've already talked myself into."

"We don't mind in the least," I said.

"But I wanted you to see what I'm doing, and what I plan to do," he continued. "Besides, you can chalk me up as a convert. In fact I'd like to be the first pledge on your website – Forrest Woodland pledges to make the core of his business the employment of the unemployable. That has a nice ring to it, don't you think."

"A beautiful ring," Arthur told him. "But I should warn you, it won't be easy. Most of these people are going to be suffering a mental illness, and it's hard to even get them out of the blocks."

"Of course it's hard. But no harder than what Pete's doing. Just remember there is nothing money, determination and ingenuity can't achieve." Then he turned to Manny: "Isn't that right, Manny?"

"Yes, Forrest," Manny replied, and maybe he looked just a little more convinced this time.

"Can I ask why you've chosen to go this way?" I asked.

"These people are my neighbors," Forrest

said. "Just like the Aborigines are my neighbors up in the Kimberley. And you love your neighbor, don't you? It's the logical place to start."

"You sound like you might be a religious man," Arthur said.

"Actually I'm not. But I'm always open to a good idea. Come on let's go back to the Frisco and I'll buy us a beer to celebrate." Then he thought for a moment. "Better idea, let's go over to the cocktail bar at The Blue. I'm meeting the New South Wales Minister for Housing there later anyway. Want to see if I can get some public housing for my hobos."

"Do you think you have a chance?" I asked.

"None at all," he laughed. "But we need to go through the motions. You just never know. Besides, every stride toward success demands a dozen pointless steps into the quagmire. Let's go to The Blue. We can see how the other half lives."

So we accompanied Forrest Woodland down to one of Sydney's most exclusive hotels where he bought us the most extravagant cocktails we had ever seen at the most extravagant prices. We toasted all our future endeavors, and three-quarters of an hour later Arthur and I were back on the street near where we had started, feeling a little drunk and quite satisfied with our first venture. I suggested we have a coffee to sober up.

We sat down at a cafe on the side of the Finger Wharf next to the Marina. No sooner had we ordered than I noticed some people disembark from one of the luxury yachts about 100 yards up the wharf. As they emerged onto the boardwalk I recognized one of the group.

"This is amazing," I said to Arthur, "see that little guy in the dark suit. That's our other Aussie. That's John Stockton."

"Stinky Stockton?"

"The same. He always holidays in Oz over Christmas."

"Then it's fate," Arthur said with enthusiasm. "It's Kismet. Let's go for it."

"But we haven't formally approached him..." I began.

But Arthur was up, out of his seat and heading for Stinky. Stockton was walking towards Arthur, with a woman beside him who was taking notes as he spoke, and two body guards, one next to him, one next to the woman. In the short space of time it took to rise and go after Arthur, I couldn't help reflecting how antithetical he was to Forrest in every aspect of his dress and demeanor.

Arthur reached the group while I was still a way back, but I saw him hold out his hand to Stockton and I could just hear him introduce himself. I saw Stockton not respond to the handshake and stand there looking at him. Arthur began trying to explain who we were and why we wanted to talk to him. Stockton looked at his body guards, one of whom started to move towards Arthur. I rushed forward.

"I'm really sorry to disturb you, Mr Stockton,"

I said. "Let me just explain…"

"I know who you are and what you're doing," he said, and his tone was not welcoming. "I expected you to harass me at some point, but hoped you would go through channels. This is my private time."

I couldn't help reflecting how these rich guys were always so well informed. Max knew all about us. So did Forrest. Now so too did Stockton, though clearly his information gathering had been to keep us at bay.

"I really am sorry," I said. "We should have gone through channels. Next time…"

"There will be no next time," Stockton said, and brushed past me.

So of course I had no choice but to let it go. Unfortunately Arthur didn't see things the same way. Whether it was enthusiasm or alcohol or both, he hadn't quite picked up on the tone of the moment.

"But don't you think, seeing we're all here now…", he began as he walked after Stockton. The security guard who had already moved close to Arthur, just stuck out his very long arm (which was attached to a very large body), and stopped Arthur's forward motion by seizing the back of his collar.

"Hang on a minute," I said, but before I could say more, the guard had lifted Arthur off the ground by the collar, carried him the few steps to the edge of the wharf and dropped him in the

Harbour. It took me a moment to believe what I had just seen. I glanced at Stockton who was continuing down the boardwalk dictating notes to his secretary again. The other body guard had gone with them. I just stood there confronted by a smiling gorilla who had just peremptorily thrown my friend in the drink.

I saw red. As ludicrous as it now seems, I rushed at the guard. I wanted to hurt him. I wanted to avenge my friend. Clearly all sense of reality had abandoned me. My flaying fists did not even touch his coat sleeves. Before I knew it he had spun me round, picked me up in the same fashion used on Arthur, and consigned me to Arthur's exact fate.

We bobbed together at the foot of the iron ladder which luckily led down from the wharf to the water near where we had been thrown in. As we both grabbed the ladder, Arthur said:

"It's kind of like the inverse of when you jumped in to save Max."

"Kind of," I agreed.

And then we both began to giggle uncontrollably. It was not the alcohol. We had definitely sobered up. But the ludicrousness of the situation had decided to impress itself upon us.

As we reached the top of the ladder, a helping hand was held out to us. We saw the smiling face of Forrest Woodland. He started to giggle too, and soon the three of us were standing on the boardwalk laughing uncontrollably. When we had settled a little Forrest turned to a man we hadn't even noticed was there.

"I'd like you to meet the Minister for Housing for the State of New South Wales," he said, and we realized we were being snapped by a photographer who had come to the meeting between the Minister and Forrest.

The next day we were on the front page of The Sydney Morning Herald, Arthur and I looking bedraggled but amused, Forrest looking delighted, and the Minister looking like he just didn't know how to react.

Of course the story got in papers around the world, how Stinky Stockton had two of Pete A. Vanderveer's top executives unceremoniously pitched into Sydney Harbour.

Pete wanted to sue Stockton. But I said no. It would be pointless. Besides, the publicity was giving us a real start on our work. If anyone amongst the wealthy didn't know about us before, they certainly did now. Interestingly too, it opened doors for us. We found, perhaps not surprisingly, that Stinky had more enemies than friends. His treatment of us endeared us to a lot of people.

So began a two year odyssey for Arthur and myself. We found ourselves in China, Europe, Russia and in all parts of the Americas. Sometimes, we would be on a plane or sitting in the waiting room of some huge multi-national, and I would look across at Arthur and remember how we shared a space on the porch of Sts Peter and Paul Church in Boulder Colorado. And I would marvel at the twists and turns life is capable of taking

It was exciting, it was edifying, and it was exhausting. But by the end of the two years nearly a third of the Top 200 Billionaires had made a public commitment to go the way of Pete and Katherine and Max

I wasn't sure whether those commitments would necessarily bear fruit, but Max was convinced they would. He was sure that in their hearts those who made a promise were going to be like Forrest and himself, people who wanted, and probably had always wanted, to make this the center of their lives.

After all, Max pointed out, they weren't politicians. They didn't need to make promises, unless they meant to keep them. It might take a few years. It might take a couple of decades.

"But it's going to happen," he said. "That I can guarantee you. When the time is right and the Board approves and the customers are ready, they'll all come through. And they won't be the last. One day the way of Pete and Katherine will just be the way it's done."

It was wonderful to hear. It helped us find the energy to go on. And if it were just hard work that the future held, I think I would have found the energy to go on a lot longer. But for all the joy and excitement of this wonderful job, there was always a part of me that was 'slowed' by the presence of

Katherine in it all. I was like an athlete with a tiny stone in his shoe.

I just couldn't escape my feelings, and I just couldn't escape her. Not that I really wanted to. I loved her. I loved to see her. But when I did, the old yearning was always there. Sure I was on the road most of the time. But whenever I was back in New York, there she was. And she would call all the time, because she was an executive of the company and she cared about what was happening. Indeed as time went by she became more and more interested in what Arthur and I were doing.

I would be at dinner in Tel Aviv, or being driven to a meeting in Beijing, and I would take a call from her. Then all the old emotions would shoot straight to the surface again, just as powerful as they had ever been.

I just couldn't understand why there was no diminution. It wasn't like me to hold a candle for someone who didn't reciprocate my feelings. I kept waiting for things to change but they never did. After a time I began to think there was something more I needed to understand. There had to be a last piece of the puzzle I needed to find.

I was right. There was one more piece, and it would explain the intensity of the emotion which was always with me. But the picture that last piece revealed, was going to be more than I could look at.

19.

It was the combination of alcohol and exhaustion which did it. We had been out celebrating with the champagne king Jean-Pierre Pujadas, who was moving past the commitment stage and into action. We were in a bar somewhere in Midtown. It think it was called Purgatory, which was kind of appropriate for how I felt.

I had watched Katherine for most of the night, as she chatted so easily and so beautifully with our guest and with Max. I realized it was her belief, her commitment which underpinned everything we did. It was the belief she had when I first saw her and first fell in love with her in Sri Lanka.

Lots of people grow up believing the world can be changed for the better. Few resist the decline into cynicism. But Katherine seemed incapable of that. There she had much in common with Marjorie. But whereas Marjorie dealt with the problem in front of her, Katherine had the vision. She saw beyond the moment to what *could* be done.

I realized then how much I loved the goodness which glowed in her. It was an uncompromising goodness, as I had discovered that first day in Sri Lanka. A gentle, uncompromising goodness. It was what I had fallen in love with. No doubt it was what Pete had fallen in love with. And it was what all who met her loved, including Max and Marjorie and tonight Jean-Pierre.

As always, as I watched her, I suffered the mixed emotion of love and resentment. The resentment wasn't with her (at least I hoped not), but with a fate which never gave me a chance. I hated that feeling. I hated the fisticuffs that feeling and I engaged in every time she was around. I never did work out how to stop it, how to deal with it, apart from ordering another drink.

Around ten o'clock the party started to break up and I rose to leave, but Katherine said:

"Stay for one more, will you, Joe? There's something I want to ask you."

So we sat side by side on a couch against the wall. It had no support at all, so I felt like I was in a beanbag. It didn't help my mood, to be exhausted and drunk in Purgatory, and now feeling I was sinking down into the ninth circle. Katherine didn't seem to notice my discomfort. She was happy and had ideas on her mind.

"I love this part of the business. I mean your part of the business. When you see someone like Jean-Pierre start to come round. I really enjoy being a part of that."

"I'm glad," I said.

"You know what I'd really like?"

"What?"

"If I could go with you and Arthur sometimes,

you know, when you're off to see one of these people for the first time. I'd love to be part of the 'first contact' just occasionally. What do you reckon, Joe, would you mind if I did that sometimes?"

And then it all came out. My frustration from all the years of wanting her, and not being able to have her, of having to go on the road and become a hobo just to escape her, and having to come back into the fold despite all the difficulties, just because it was the right thing to do. They all seemed to funnel down into that horrible beanbag like couch. I struggled to get out, and as I finally freed myself, I stood before her and just yelled:

"Yes I do mind! No you can't come!"

I'm not sure whether my yelling shocked Katherine or myself the most. But there I stood, in silence, looking down on her, sunk, like I had just been, in the beanbag couch.

"Did I do something to upset you?" she asked, confused, timid.

That beautiful innocence should have brought me to a shuddering halt. But it didn't. The genie was out of the bottle, and he was going to take his chance. He was going to tell Katherine just how cramped and uncomfortable that bottle had been all these years.

"Yes you did something to upset me," I said, loudly, though not quite as loudly as before. "You always have. You bloody well always will."

"You had better tell me about this, Joe," she

said, holding out her hand, so I could hoist her from the couch.

"I'll tell you. I'll bloody well tell you!" I said, as I wrenched her up.

We stood there inches apart, she looking sad and confused, me no doubt looking like some escapee from the other side of the Styx.

"Ok," she said. "But let's sit somewhere more solid."

As soon as we did, I leaned right across with my elbows on the table, and my fists pushed tightly into the side of my face. The genie was trying to hold himself together.

"I fell in love with you while you were still talking!" I grunted. "How ridiculous is that? I never believed in love at first sight. But there it was. You on your feet at that reception in Sri Lanka, telling me I was a tight arse. And still I fell in love with you. So in love I couldn't even hear what you said.

"And when I was down on the ground with you on top of me and the bullets flying everywhere, all I could think was: 'I hope this is Katherine'. No thought about the fact that I might die. I just wanted it to be you. How absurd is that?"

She went to speak, but the genie wasn't finished.

"But you know the really absurd thing, so much more absurd than all the years of yearning after you, having to leave the company because I couldn't bear to be around you, becoming a hobo and a street performer, just to stay away from you? The really absurd thing is that you have no feelings for me. Never did have. Never will have. That's what really pisses me off."

We sat silently for a long time, looking at each other. Amidst my fury, of course, I still loved her and that made things so much worse.

"Ah," she said finally.

"Yes indeed, ah! Well may you say ah!"

"It's not true," she said finally.

"I can assure you it's all true," I told her in no uncertain terms. "That is just how I've felt and no doubt always will."

"I mean it's not true I never had feelings for you."

Sometimes words are so alien they just won't go in. This was just such a moment. I might have expected almost anything from Katherine. But not that. I must have worn a strange look indeed.

"You know I love Pete, and nothing is going to change that?" she said. I nodded. "But when you and I were first together, I certainly had feelings for you, strong feelings, which could have taken us anywhere."

After an impossibly long moment:

"Why didn't you say something?" My bellowing voice had become a sad whisper.

"Because I wasn't sure how you felt, and I didn't want to compromise you. You had offered the charity lots of money. I didn't want you to think I was just after more. Why didn't *you* say something?"

"Because I didn't think there was anything there, on your part. I cared for you. I didn't want to offend you, didn't want to make you uncomfortable. Then Pete came along."

Again we were silent. Finally Katherine said: "I guess we were both wrong."

"There's wrong and then there's *very* wrong. You are the former. I am the latter." It was of course totally impossible to pin down any of the crazy melange of emotions I felt right then, but one idea did manage to intrude its way into my mind. "Maybe it explains one thing," I said. "I've never understood how my feelings for you could just keep going when they weren't returned. That's not like me. But maybe if you know, somewhere deep down, that it hasn't been totally one-sided..."

I couldn't finish. But I'd made my point. I'd made all my points. Now I was left back where I was, only if possible, with things more difficult than they had ever been. Once again I was reminded how differently people can see the same situation. Once again I was reminded how dire the consequences of that can be.

"What are you going to do, Joe?" Katherine asked. Her voice was charged with a compassion that made things better and worse all at the same time.

"I don't know," I said. "I have new-found

knowledge. But I don't think it's going to help."

20.

I didn't sleep that night, and next day felt perhaps as lost as I had ever been. As I sat trying to make myself eat some breakfast, I had no idea what to do. Then of course it came to me. I needed to see Marjorie. I tried to make myself look presentable, and went to find her in her office.

"I've seen you look better," she said.

Then, standing on the other side of her desk, I poured out everything that happened with Katherine the night before. I was still in some sort of shock, I told her.

"How do you feel about Katherine now?" she asked.

"I feel she is a wonderful person who has never done anything that isn't perfectly correct."

"Do you still love her?"

"Of course."

"How do you feel about yourself?"

"I feel like I missed my chance," I said, and to my own surprise felt the tears start to run down my cheek.

We were in Marjorie's office. She went quickly to close the door. That was my signal to really blubber. The Bra Boy, lifeguard, rugby player started to blubber. The last time that had happened I was seven years old and my father told me Bra Boys don't cry. So I never did. Till now. Marjorie took my head in her hands and let me cry. When I was finished, I managed to ask, in a voice that could have been that seven year old:

"What should I do now?"

I saw that Marjorie had tears in her eyes too:

"I love you very much, and this is hard to say. But I think you should go home."

"To Buffalo?"

"No," she smiled, "to Australia."

"Why?"

"Because it's time. For most people a time comes when they need to go home. I think this is your time."

"Shouldn't I just try to get past it? When you wanted me to come back, you said I should just try to get past it."

"That was before we knew how Katherine once felt. That makes a difference, I think."

"Doesn't that just make it harder? Don't I just have to work harder to get past it?"

"Maybe sometimes, if you love somebody enough, and you know they may have loved you, maybe you're not supposed to get past it."

Those words sunk deep. I knew she was right. Still I said:

"What about my job. Who will do my job?"

"I imagine Arthur would do it well enough."

"Arthur was better at it than me," I said. "Besides Katherine wants to be involved and she'll be brilliant."

"Problem solved then."

"But what would I do in Australia?" I asked.

"A man with your experience could do almost anything," she said. "We know people out there. We could set you up. Merchant banking, publishing, something in government supplies." I winced. She laughed at my reaction and said: "I don't know. Whatever you fancy. It doesn't really matter much." Then with a twinkle in her eye she added: "You could become a shoeshine. Throw away your false teeth and run a shoeshine business."

I laughed: "Not really in my skill set."

I walked to the window and looked down over New York City. I didn't want to leave it. I wasn't sure Australia really was my home anymore. I'd had one brief trip there, not so long ago, and ended up in Sydney Harbour. Still, Stinky Stockton was hardly typical of the nation in which I had grown up.

"Maybe I could work for Forrest Woodland," I suggested.

"Or at least work the way he works. What did he say: 'Love thy neighbor?' It's what you've been doing for a long time now anyway."

It was a beautiful thing for Marjorie to say. It was always her way, to look for a kindness to give.

"I wonder who my neighbor will be, back in Oz?" I asked, still looking down on the Avenue of the Americas.

"I can't tell you that, but I do know your neighbor is the person you can reach out and touch. If you are a bum sleeping on the porch of a church, your neighbor is the person sleeping next to you. If you are a billionaire you can pretty much touch the world."

She paused, and I turned back to her. She was looking at me with such love it is impossible for me to describe.

"Each to his own, Joe. You give according to your bounty. You have stood in the shoes of billionaires and you have touched the world. Now maybe it's time to shine a few shoes. Shine them well though. Make sure people can see their own reflections in the shoes you shine."

21.

This time I was not going to run away. I was going to say goodbye to the people who mattered to me.

I started with Max. I'm not sure why. Maybe because he was the newest person in my life, and thus easier to leave than the people I loved so much. Maybe because I figured he would be the least likely to try and talk me out of it. He did respect my decision. But the parting was harder than I imagined, perhaps because he said:

"If a person saves your life, they go into a special box. You don't want to have to open it and let them fly away."

"You'll come and see me in Australia," I said. "You can afford the fare."

"Can I? Isn't Australia just too far away?"

"They have several eccentric billionaires there. Forrest Woodland is already doing some great work."

"I'll look forward to meeting him."

"Arthur will have to go back soon. You can hitch a ride with him."

"Will Arthur run the show?"

"That's the idea. If he agrees."

He thought for a minute and said: "Yes, he'll do a good job." Then he said: "What will you do?"

"I don't know. Marjorie thinks I should be a shoeshine."

"Can't quite see that," he laughed. "Is this whole thing her idea? I'll have to give her a talking to."

"It's not exactly her idea. It's just that when I speak with her she tells me the things I'm thinking, the ones I haven't yet realized I'm thinking."

Max shook his head: "Tell me you're not going to cut up your credit cards, and give away all your money to the Foundation again."

"I'm going to cut up my credit cards and give my money to the Foundation. I'll keep enough to buy the brushes and polish," I laughed.

"Is there any way you can make me understand the need for this drama?"

"I don't think so," I smiled. "But I'll set Arthur the task. He's a great dramaturg."

Max and I shook hands then. He looked sad. That made it hard. Nonetheless it was a good feeling to know I had touched a man of his caliber.

After seeing Max, I spent time alone in my office. The whole process had been harder than I expected, which meant my next visit was going to be a whole lot harder still. Nonetheless, after about an hour spent working up the courage, I walked down the corridor to Pete's office. He was waiting for me.

"You are the most unreliable employee this company has ever had," he smiled. He had obviously decided to keep this light. But before I could even answer, his resolve vanished. He banged his fist on the desk and said: "Damn it! It's just not fair."

"*Life* is not fair," I told him. "But we can still do some good along the way."

"What? Shining shoes?" he almost barked at me, then hung his head.

"Enlisting billionaires. Shining shoes. Yes, things like that."

"I suppose you won't tell me this time either?" he accused.

From that I realized neither Katherine nor Marjorie had told him what was driving me away, yet again. I was glad of that. It still would achieve nothing and just expose Pete to unnecessary hurt.

"No, Pete, I'm sorry. The Bra Boy stands mute yet again."

"Damn Bra Boys!" he scowled.

"Come out to Sydney," I suggested. "I'll introduce you to a mob of them, all much more unreliable than me."

Then to my absolute amazement he rushed over and threw his arms around me. It was totally out of character for him, totally out of character for us. I was so shocked I just stood there for a moment whilst he squeezed my body, at a loss what to do. Then I realized I just needed to hug him back, which I did.

For a long moment we were locked together. Then he broke away and stood there, his head down. I touched him gently on the arm and left the room.

By now I was physically and emotionally exhausted. But I felt if I didn't push on, I would never have the courage to see everyone and tell them what I felt. So I went to Marjorie's office next. As I came through the door I instinctually pulled it closed behind me. Maybe I knew I would blubber again.

And I did. All I said was "thank you" and I was off. The seven year old was back. Eventually I pulled myself together and we began to talk of smaller things. Everything that mattered had already been said. We talked of Sydney too. She had never been there, and promised she would visit and let me take her on a tour. For the first time then I started to get just a little excited at the thought of going home.

"It could be fun," I said. "Going home. It could be an adventure."

"It will certainly be both," she assured me. Then she asked: "Who have you seen?"

"Max and Pete."

"Can I make a suggestion? Leave Arthur till tomorrow. And definitely leave Katherine for a little while yet."

I took Marjorie's advice. I kissed her goodbye, then went straight home, fell on the bed and slept till morning. Then I went to see Arthur.

"What an amazing time we've had," he said to me as I came through the door of his office. "I can tell you honestly, Joe, the semi-official promenade street theater troupe was better than anything I ever did Off-Broadway. Better by a mile."

"It might just be the best thing I *ever* did," I told him in all sincerity.

"And the chance to work with you," he continued, "to go all over the world and meet all those amazing people. That was almost as good." He laughed. "I hear you're going to shine shoes. I might try something similar. In Boulder I think. It was always my favorite place to be a hobo."

"Haven't they told you?" I asked.

"Told me what?"

"You're going to take over from me. Run the show."

"I can't do that." He was recoiling before my eyes. "Not without you. Not at all, in fact."

"Listen, Arthur," I said, coming over and putting both my hands on his shoulders, which was out of character for us too. But I wanted to make my point. "The only reason I can do what I have to do, is because I know you'll do a better job than I ever did. Don't let me down."

"But, but…"

"I'll miss you too," I said. "But come out to Oz. I promise to keep you out of the Harbour this time."

In some ways leaving Arthur was the hardest of all. We had been inseparable, in so many guises, for so many years. It was near impossible to imagine a world where he wouldn't always be there. After I left his office I was totally drained. I went and sat on a bench in the park beneath our office. I needed air. I also needed to work out what I was going to say to Katherine. I just had no idea.

I had been down in the street nearly two hours and yet was no closer to working out what to say to the woman who had filled so much of my emotional life over so many years. Then, all of a sudden, for some reason, it dawned on me. I had already said everything I needed to say, everything I had always wanted to say, that night in the bar in Purgatory. Katherine would know I was leaving, and why I was leaving. There was, quite literally, nothing more to tell her.

Then before the thought had even settled, she

was sitting beside me.

"I've been watching you from my office window," she said, "sitting here struggling with yourself."

"Am I that obvious?"

"It's just that you've seen everyone else, and said what you had to say, and I'm thinking I must be next. I am next aren't I?"

"Yes of course you are."

"But I want you to stop struggling. You don't need to work out what to say to me. Nor do I need to work out what to say to you. We said it all in Purgatory."

"I just realized that," I told her, "just before you sat down."

Then she thought for a minute. She was obviously struggling with whether to speak. Finally she said:

"It's not totally true, though. There is one more thing I want to say. I'm not sure if I should, but I will."

"Please. Say it."

"I would have liked us to grow old together in this wonderful work we're doing. I am unbearably sad it cannot be."

She touched something then, at the very core of me. It was so true and it went so deep, I just couldn't respond. All I could do was take her hand and hold it while we sat there in silence. After what seemed like a very long time, I got up, and she got up too. Then I kissed her, turned to the street, hailed a taxi and left her, my Australian friend, there in New York City.

Somehow, out of the blur of emotion, I found myself at the airport. I was hours too early, and just sat in the gate lounge staring at whatever afternoon television had to offer that day, soundless and inane.

In fact it was probably the television which started to move me back into the real world. Whatever pain I was feeling, whatever confusion I suffered, nothing could be as bad as that television.

As I walked, I moved through a rapid sequence of emotions, from confusion to optimism to despair and back again. Fortunately, though I had no confidence it would prevail, my dominant emotion seemed to be optimism. I was going home. It had been a long time. It was exciting, it could even be an adventure. I had a whole new life ahead of me.

After a while I realized I had been pacing back and forth right in front of a shoeshine stand. I smiled to myself. For a time I watched that honest artisan toiling away. Then I sat down and had a shine. The shoe shiner worked slowly and methodically. We chatted together and his gentle voice made me feel at peace. When he had finished I looked down at my own reflection in my shoes. I remembered Marjorie's words just a few days before, though it could have been in another lifetime:

"Each to his own, Joe," she had said. "You give according to your bounty. You have stood in the shoes of billionaires and you have touched the world. Now maybe it's time to shine a few shoes. Shine them well, Joe. Make sure people can see their own reflections in the shoes you shine." '

22.

The crowd in the Pitt Street Mall had thinned. The lunchtime was over. But the crowd around the storyteller had grown. Now they all stood in silence. They watched as Joe Stalin got up and stretched. He smiled at me. I smiled back. Then the old lady with the shopping trolley came up beside me and gently touched me on the arm.

'Does that answer your question, Vic?' she asked.

ABOUT THE AUTHOR

Victor Kline started his working life as Sydney's youngest barrister. He worked as a Federal prosecutor, and later as a defense counsel in the Northern Territory in its Wild West days. These days he is back in Sydney, concentrating on Human Rights and Refugee law. In between he has been a playwright, theater director and actor, off-Broadway and in various parts of Australia. He is also the author of the novel *Rough Justice* and the bestselling memoir *The House at Anzac Parade*. As well as New York and Central Australia, Victor has lived and worked in London, Paris, the South of France and New Guinea. He now lives on the Lower North Shore, with wife Katharine and a little grey cat called Spud.